"First, raise your knees and plant your feet wide..."

Obeying Clay's instructions, Gabby's thighs touched his butt.

"Now move your left wrist away from your head." He demonstrated the self-defense move slowly. "See? That throws me off balance because my hand goes out from under me."

"Oh, cool. Let me try that again."

Now she was on her back and he was above her. Chest to chest. With only the thin cotton of their shirts between them. His hardness pressed to her softness. Everywhere.

She took a deep breath and licked her lips. His eyes were a whiskey brown. His mouth... She wanted to lift her head and catch it with her own. Just to see if it was as supple as it looked.

She wasn't expecting till death did them part. But before she returned to reality, at the very least, she wanted a kiss. Mostly to see if kissing him was as amazing as she remembered.

She claimed his lips then. And after a stunned second, he returned her kiss, his mouth moving over hers, nipping, tasting.

Needing him, she clasped his jaw, tangled her fingers in his hair. She was drowning in the feel of his mouth on hers, taking and giving, plundering. She started untucking his shirt and inching it up his back, running her palms over the hot, bare skin...

She refused to lose this moment. She would have him once and for all.

Dear Reader,

When Harlequin asked me for more Uniformly Hot! romances, I knew I wanted to write about Navy SEALs and immediately began researching everything about them. There are a lot of great books about Special Ops and the Navy SEALs in particular. Information concerning actual missions, weapons and tactics, as well as the grueling training. Learning about their everyday lives and challenges was fascinating and definitely inspired my fictional hero, Clay Bellamy.

Unlike many true SEALs, however, Clay is not a family man. His childhood made him a cynic when it comes to love. He's certainly never known a woman as innocent and kindhearted as Gabriella Diaz. She desperately needs his help and I hope you enjoy their wild, sexy journey to love.

Researching SEALs also led me to the Navy SEAL Foundation, navysealfoundation.org. I've made a contribution already and will be making more with each royalty check from this book. Consider donating if you can and please visit my website, jillianburns.com, for information on my next book.

Sincerely,

Jillian

Jillian Burns

Her SEAL Protector

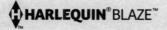

Recycling programs
for this product may
not exist in your area.

ISBN-13: 978-0-373-79908-4

Her SEAL Protector

Copyright © 2016 by Juliet L. Burns

Printed in U.S.A.

www.Harlequin.com

Jillian Burns fell in love while reading such classics as *Jane Eyre* and *Pride and Prejudice* in her teens and has been reading romance novels ever since. She lives in Texas with her husband of twenty-five years and their three half-grown kids. She likes to think her emotional nature—sometimes referred to as moodiness by those closest to her—has found the perfect outlet in writing stories filled with passion and romance. She believes romance novels have the power to change lives with their message of eternal love and hope.

Books by Jillian Burns

Harlequin Blaze

Let It Ride
Seduce and Rescue
Primal Calling
By Invitation Only
"Secret Encounter"
Relentless Seduction
Cabin Fever

Uniformly Hot!

Night Maneuvers
Once a Hero...
Fevered Nights

To Michael Monsoor, hero Navy SEAL who gave his life for his fellow SEALs, and for all US soldiers who put themselves in harm's way for their country. You are the true heroes.

If you would like to help veterans overcome their challenges, or "Charlie Mike," please visit missioncontinues.org.

Acknowledgments

Thanks to Scott and Brian for generously letting me use your apartment as the inspiration for Gabby's. And a special thank-you to my sister from another mother, Debrah Huston Coward, for loaning me all your wonderful books about Navy SEALs. I'll get them back to you soon, I promise!

Once again I couldn't have produced this without the usual suspects: Pam, Linda, Von and Barb. And thank you to the best editor anyone could wish for.

1

@nerdybankanalyst
I'm sad conference is over but had amazing time. Still, no place like home #paraguayconference

"Excuse me." Mr. Van Horton tapped Gabby on the shoulder as she finished her Tweet. "Could you—" he pointed at the bags of luggage sitting beside him "—find a porter, *por favor*?"

Gabby sighed inwardly. This was the third time in as many days that someone from her own office had mistaken her for a hotel employee. It was understandable, she supposed. Especially now that, with the conference over, everyone was scrambling to check out and get home. And her plain black suit jacket and skirt looked similar to the hotel employees' uniforms. Mr. Van Horton had probably seen her speaking in Spanish to the hotel manager a moment ago, thanking the woman for the excellent accommodations on behalf of all the New York Corporate Bank Inc. people during their stay in Paraguay.

But most likely her Hispanic heritage caused him to mistake her for a local.

Still, she'd worked at the bank for almost two years. Seeing the executives in the break room, passing them in the hallways. She'd even sat in on a meeting with Mr. Van Horton once.

She should say something. She *was* going to say something this time. She drew in a deep breath. Squared her shoulders.

But... Mr. Van Horton was the executive vice president. Did it really matter if he didn't know who she was? Maybe she—

"Do you speak English?" Mr. Van Horton spoke slower and louder. "Find a porter?" He gestured at his luggage again and glanced at the registration desk, then back at her.

The deep breath of determination deflated. "Yes, sir." Gabby turned toward the concierge's desk.

"Sir." James Pender blocked her path. He nodded at the Executive VP and gestured toward Gabby. "You know Gabriella Diaz, our newest credit risk analyst?" James winked at her as Mr. Van Horton's eyes widened and his mouth opened and shut like the white bass she'd once caught on the Guadalupe River.

"Oh, of course, I'm sorry, Ms. Diaz." Mr. V recovered with a strained smile. "I didn't recognize you."

"We've never been introduced." Gabby could feel her cheeks heat. "I'll get a porter for you, sir." Wishing she could disappear, she stepped to the concierge's desk and arranged to have Mr. V's luggage taken out to a waiting cab.

Despite being colleagues in the same department, until this moment Gabby hadn't thought James Pender even knew she existed.

After thanking the hotel manager once again, she rolled her own suitcase out to the hotel drive just as Mr. Van Horton was getting into a cab.

She dabbed at her temples with the back of her hand. February *was* summertime in South America, but even so, the weather was sweltering. Still, it beat the freezing temps back in New York. She shivered thinking of the dirty snow and slush she'd most likely return to. If only she'd had more time to explore the beautiful city of Asunción.

"Ms. Diaz!" Mr. Van Horton waved her over. "You and James share my cab."

Gabby glanced over to see James wheeling his suitcase to a stop beside hers. He mugged a "why not?" face and proceeded to load his bag into the cab's trunk.

"Come on, Ms. Diaz." Mr. Van Horton waved at her again with a winking smile. "I should get to know my newest credit risk analyst."

Gabby drew a deep breath. Get to know her? Anxiety set in at being the center of attention. He was probably just feeling guilty about his mistake. But if she declined, he might think she was holding it against him. There was no hope for it. Resigned, she rolled her bag to the trunk. James had taken the front seat, so she slid into the backseat beside Mr. V.

As the cab pulled away from the hotel, Gabby

glanced back at the unforgettable mountain vista behind the hotel. Definitely the best perk of her job. Just
in the last eighteen months she'd traveled to Los An-
geles, Miami and now Paraguay. Of course, that probably had more to do with her bilingual skills than her
risk-analysis savvy, but it all helped her career. The
raise last month had gone straight to Jorge's college
fund. And once her brother graduated next year, she
could start helping Patricia.

"So, how do you feel the conference went, Ms. Diaz?"

Gabby turned her attention inside the cab and found
Mr. Van Horton studying her intently. She swallowed
and glanced at James, who had half turned from the
front seat to face them, smiling encouragingly. She
cleared her throat. "The workshop on financial global-
ization in a nonrisk asset world was very interesting."

Mr. Van Horton's eyes narrowed. "I highly doubt
that." Then he grinned. "Tell me you at least saw some
of the sights while you were here. Have you ever been
out of the country before?"

"No, sir."

"Now, none of that sirring me. Call me Bob."

Oh, she couldn't picture herself calling him Bob.
Gabby gave a shy smile.

"How about you?" Mr. Van Horton addressed James,
who proceeded to chatter on about the amenities of the
hotel, the nightclub he'd been to the night before and a
quick rundown of the lectures he'd attended.

The cab screeched to a stop, throwing Gabby against
the back of the driver's seat. An explosion of gunfire
roared around her. Shattered glass sprayed over her, and

she screeched and covered her head. Before she could comprehend what was happening, a man wrenched her door open and shouted in Spanish for her to get out.

Gabby couldn't move. Couldn't think. The bandit reached in, yanked her out of the cab and dragged her toward an old Jeep. Mr. V was pulled out of the other side and shoved beside her. The cabdriver was cowering on the ground next to the car.

The lower halves of the attackers' faces were covered with bandannas and they all carried big automatic rifles.

James scrambled out on his own and stuck his hands in the air as one of the gunmen poked his rifle in James's stomach. "Throw out your phones!" the gunman yelled in heavily accented English.

James and Mr. V both fished in their coat pockets and tossed their phones away.

A second gunman found her purse on the cab's floor, dumped it and smashed her phone with the butt of his rifle.

The bandit closest to Mr. V yelled at them in Spanish to get in the Jeep.

"What are they saying, Ms. Diaz?" Mr. Van Horton whispered to her.

"No hablar!" The gunman jabbed the butt of his rifle into Mr. Van Horton's stomach and he doubled over.

Gabby bit off a scream.

"In!" The gunmen shouted again, waved the rifle toward the Jeep and this time he shot at the ground in front of them.

Gabby screamed and James, his face twisted in terror, jumped into the back. Gabby was shaking so hard she had to try twice to get a good enough grip to pull herself into the Jeep. But Mr. Van Horton didn't follow.

"Speak English?" He addressed one of the gunmen. "I have money. No need to take us. I can—"

With an expression of pure hatred, the thug bashed Mr. Van Horton in the head this time and he collapsed to the ground. The men picked him up and threw him into the back of the Jeep, got in the front and sped off.

Blood gushed from Mr. V's head. So much blood. She shrugged out of her suit coat and tore it into a makeshift compress. "James, hold this while I take off his tie."

"What?" He was shaking uncontrollably.

"We've got to stop the bleeding. Keep pressure on the wound."

James just stared at her.

With a *tsk* of exasperation, she reached over and placed his hand on the bandage. "Press hard." Then she loosened Mr. V's tie and used it to hold the compress.

She kept a close eye on Mr. V as they bumped along in the rusty Jeep. It seemed like hours as they climbed into the mountains. Even if she'd wanted to jump out, the kidnappers kept a gun trained on them. And she couldn't leave Mr. V, who still hadn't woken up.

The heat was relentless until they entered the shade of the jungle, and even then, the humidity pressed in on them. By the time they came to a stop, Gabby was soaked in sweat, she was dying of thirst and she really had to relieve herself. But all of that ceased to matter as they dragged her, James and Mr. V into a hut in the middle of nowhere and tied them up.

Somewhere along the way James had become catatonic. Mr. V still hadn't regained consciousness. And she wasn't sure any of them were going to get out of this alive.

"You ready?" L.T., Clay's lieutenant, asked in a low voice.

Petty Officer Clay Bellamy gave L.T. the thumbs-up, and then waited for the signal to go.

L.T. radioed to Main that they were going in, asking for confirmation on the extract location.

Clay's SEAL team had parachuted into the mountains of Paraguay last night, landed in a clearing, then traveled for miles on foot through a dense jungle to set up position half a click from the target. Their mission: personnel recovery. Three United States civilians held by unknown assailants.

Intel was sketchy but they didn't think this was the work of the local cartel. The Americans were bankers, and the international bank they worked for had received a ransom demand via Twitter two days ago. Which, hopefully, meant the civvies were still alive. But hostages were rarely left alive after a ransom was paid. And just because this might not be a cartel didn't mean that the kidnappers weren't armed to the teeth.

Clay's lieutenant squeezed his shoulder and Clay rose from his squat and sprinted toward the back of the dilapidated hut, staying low.

L.T. maintained his position hidden in the foliage to communicate with Main, while Bull—positioned at nine o'clock—kept his silenced M40 trained on the two guards by the door of the hut.

Clay gave the signal that his team was in position. Through his scope, Bull shot both guards. Doughboy and Chipper sped around the corner and caught them as they fell to prevent the thump of dropping bodies from alerting anyone inside. Clay grabbed the guards' phones and guns, and then gave the signal for a hard entry.

They burst through the door and Chipper shot the guy sitting at a table just as he aimed his gun.

Spreading out, they checked the other two rooms, calling out "clear" as each was found empty. Damn. The hostages weren't here. And where were the rest of the kidnappers? They weren't hiding outside. His team had been watching the area for hours before dawn and would've spotted them.

If he'd had any, the hair on Clay's neck would've stood up. "Cover me," he ordered Doughboy and Chipper, then, staying low, ran outside to what he'd assumed was a well. Basically, a two-foot-high wall of adobe surrounding a man-made hole in the ground. But now he realized what seemed off about it.

As a kid, one of his summer jobs had been cutting grass for all the neighbors and church folks. One old man—a buddy of his stepfather's—had a well on his property with a similar structure aboveground except it had been made of stones. But it had been built next to a tree and had a long rope tied around the trunk with a pail attached to the other end.

This well had no rope. No pail.

As he drew closer, Clay leaned over the adobe structure and called down into the well. "US Navy. Anybody down there?"

Silence.

He cursed under his breath and turned to head back to the hut.

Then, a faint call from below. "We're here."

It was a female voice, hoarse from dehydration no doubt, but...alive. Yes! He spun back. "How many?" He grabbed his flashlight and shone it down into the hole.

Clay could barely make out a pair of arms moving as they covered a face.

"Two," the female called.

"Can you tell me your names?" The rule was to first verify all captives.

"Gabriella Diaz and James Pender."

Identities confirmed, Clay called it in to L.T. then shouted into the well again. "Anyone need medical attention?"

The woman called up, "We're okay. But Mr. Van Horton isn't here. He was hurt. Do you have him?"

The woman sounded pretty calm considering what she must've gone through. Van Horton. Wounded and missing. Not good. "We'll get you out. Hold on."

"Don't leave us! You've got to get us out of here!" a man cried. Clay shifted the beam of light onto the other, paler hostage.

"I'm going to throw down a rope. Tie it under your arms and I'll pull you up one at a time."

Clay signaled the team. "One still missing. Search the area." Doughboy, Chipper and the rest fanned out, heading into the surrounding foliage. Clay leaned his M4 against the adobe wall, took off his pack and pulled out his length of nylon rope. With nothing else nearby to secure it to, he tied it around his waist and then tossed it down, hoping it would be long enough.

"Me first. I have to go first!" Clay heard the man in the well whine.

"There's a body partially buried out here," Chipper's voice sounded in Clay's earbud. "Caucasian. I think it's one of the hostages."

The rope jerked and Clay braced his feet against the adobe, leaned back and pulled the rope hand over hand until a tall, thin, mud-caked man appeared above the edge. His face was streaked with tear tracks as he scrabbled out and clung to Clay, sobbing.

Clay finally had to force him to let go and relinquish the rope. What kind of coward didn't let a woman go first?

Disgusted, Clay tossed the rope back down into the well. "Now you, ma'am."

Within a minute the rope tugged and Clay easily lifted the rope until a heart-shaped face appeared above the rim. Her long dark curls were a mass of tangles and her large, dark brown eyes seemed to gaze at him in disbelief. Her wide mouth trembled, though he could see she was trying to keep her lips clamped tightly together. As he pulled her up and over the edge, she landed on her feet, but her knees buckled beneath her. He caught her around the waist and she clung to his shoulders. "Sorry. I..."

"No worries. We'll have you home safe in no time."

"What about Mr. Van Hort—"

Shots fired to Clay's right and he dropped to the dirt, taking the woman with him and covering her. The man screamed and sobbed louder, cowering next to him.

"Stay here, stay down." A spray of bullets fired as Clay grabbed his M-4 and peeked over the well wall.

In his ear, L.T. was barking orders. "Q.R. coming in at one click to the south. Secure the targets and get out."

Damn. Quick response. The kidnappers weren't going to make this easy.

"Chipper's down!" Doughboy yelled into his earbud.

Shorty came hightailing it into the clearing, shooting behind him. His left arm was bleeding. Clay covered him, firing multiple rounds in the direction of the flying bullets.

As Shorty slid behind the well wall, the male hostage clutched at him. "You gotta get me out of here!"

The woman crawled over and put her arm around the guy, murmuring soothing words into his ear. Clay had to admit he wasn't sure he could've stayed that calm in her place.

L.T. barked more orders as all hell broke loose. "Our position's compromised. Go to secondary extract!"

Clay signaled to Shorty that he would lay cover while Shorty got the two hostages out. Clay was going back for Doughboy and Chipper.

Rising from his crouch, he laid down fire while Shorty grabbed the two hostages and ran for L.T.'s position. But the woman stumbled—or the male hostage shoved her as he clung to Shorty, and the fire was too heavy for Shorty to go back for her. Calling out every curse word he knew, Clay raced over and covered her with his body while firing into the foliage.

"I've got Chipper. Headed for secondary extract," Doughboy called through Clay's earbud.

One less thing to worry about. Clay scooped up the female around the waist and ran toward the exit route, but the kidnappers' truck came barreling through the brush straight for them. Taking a sharp left, Clay darted into dense undergrowth, heading for the fallback exit he'd scoped out last night. He pulled a flash-bang from his belt and pitched it behind them. Hopefully, that would slow their pursuers down.

Heedless of near impenetrable vines and shrubs, he fought through the jungle growth to put as much distance between them and the abductors as he could manage.

Gunshots popped in the distance, the sound of the trucks' engine grew fainter. The woman was keeping up on her own, so he dropped his arm and grabbed her hand instead, slowing a bit. "Follow me and stay close." From the corner of his eye he saw her nod.

Hoping the pace wasn't too much for her, he trudged farther and farther into thickening vegetation, using his M-4 to hack plants out of the way. By the time he determined gunshots had stopped and no one was following them, he was puffing out deep breaths and his camo was soaked with sweat.

He came to a halt and crouched down, and the woman crouched with him. Wiping his face on his sleeve, he tried to assess the situation. They were cut off from the rest of the team. No way they would make it to the secondary extract. Not in time. Before his team got too far out of range, he radioed L.T., confirmed their position and instructed him to send a helo to the emergency extract.

The petite woman was staring at him expectantly, but not questioning him. Her faith in his ability to get her out seemed solid. He just hoped he could prove her right.

Because they were going to have to spend the night in this jungle.

2

A SEARING PAIN burned across Gabby's back. She hadn't noticed it until this moment. The adrenaline that had seen her through the escape had vanished. But she was alive.

"We need to keep moving." Her rescuer straightened and extended a hand to help her up.

But Gabby couldn't move. She sank to her hands and knees on the wet jungle floor, shaking uncontrollably. She was paralyzed. Not with fear, or even shock. It was just…overwhelming emotion. She was alive! She was out of that disgusting hole. She was going home!

But… Mr. V. She hadn't seen him since the kidnappers had dropped her and James into that well. What if he was dead? All her bravado collapsed and she burst into tears. She couldn't help it, couldn't stop crying.

Vaguely she heard her rescuer curse and she tried to stifle the sobs. "I'm sorry."

"No, ma'am, don't you apologize." For the first time, she noticed his heavy Southern drawl. Maybe Georgia or South Carolina? But not Texas. Her own Texan twang had been remarked upon by her Northern co-workers, but this man's accent had a softer, slower cadence. Thinking about something trivial like that helped stifle her embarrassing outburst. She sniffed and before she could wipe her nose on her sleeve, he placed a large, thick green camo bandanna in her hand.

"Thank you." She cleaned her face with the bandanna, inhaling the clean, crisp laundry scent. She breathed it in and felt calmer.

The hulking soldier snapped off his helmet and crouched beside her. "Hey." He cupped her shoulder. "You're doing good. Don't worry. I'm going to get you out of here."

His eyes. They were a soft brown, so full of reassurance and concern, so incongruous with the frightening dark-green-and-black face paint and the grim set of his mouth.

"What about Mr. Van Horton? And James?" James's terror had never subsided. Inside the well it had gotten worse. Gabby had tried to comfort him as best she could, but he'd grown steadily less stable as the hours passed. "They're going to make it home, too, right?"

He nodded. "Mr. Pender is on his way to the American embassy."

"And Mr. V?"

The soldier hesitated.

Oh no. Gabby could feel her eyes sting with more tears. Mr. V was dead? She'd never known anyone who'd been murdered before. She'd tried to nurse him as best she could, asking their captors for water and medicine for his fever, but Mr. V had never regained consciousness.

"Can you get up?" The soldier slid a strong arm around her waist and she cried out.

He yanked it back, blood smeared on his palm. "What the—" He looked at his hand. "You're bleeding? You were hit?"

"I don't know." Her voice shook. She twisted to try to see and whimpered at the stab of pain.

The soldier spat out a curse word, dropped his helmet and backpack, then dug inside the pack and pulled out a first aid kit.

She'd been shot? She could feel panic rise up and choke her. She'd survived two days with homicidal kidnappers only to be shot? What if she bled to death? Mr. V was dead and now her. What if this soldier couldn't get the bullet out, or it was lodged in her spine or—

"Take off your shirt."

Gabby froze and blinked at him, but he wasn't even looking at her. He was busy pulling out a pack of wet wipes, a tube of ointment and a roll of gauze.

A wild urge to laugh bubbled up. She must be in shock. Of course the GI didn't mean anything sexual by his demand, but this wasn't exactly how she'd pictured herself undressing for a guy for the first time. Well, she wasn't panicked anymore.

"Ms. Diaz? I need to see to your injury."

"Yes. Okay." She turned away from him, forcing her fingers to undo the buttons on her formerly white silk blouse.

He helped her lower it off her shoulders and down

her arms, then she felt gentle fingers wiping something cold across the middle of her back. It stung and she tensed. There was sharp surface pain, but she didn't feel anything internal. That had to be good, right? "Is it...?"

"Just a graze. You'll be fine. I'm applying a topical antibiotic."

Just a graze. She breathed out a relieved and grateful breath.

She felt him smear some ointment on and then heard ripping paper as he pressed a bandage to her back and began winding the roll of gauze around her. His arms wrapped around her waist and his whiskered jaw grazed her cheek. He froze, the sides of his hands touching her rib cage. She sucked in and then realized that only lifted her breasts higher. He had an up close and personal view of the cleavage above her bra.

She turned her head to look at him and their gazes met.

His lips were parted and she could see that they weren't as harsh as they'd looked before. They were sensual and—they flattened as he sat back on his heels and continued wrapping the gauze around her. But when he returned to her front he very carefully kept his arms at a distance. And his gaze averted.

What would it be like to kiss those lips? What if...

"There you go." He tied off the gauze and draped her blouse across her shoulders.

What was wrong with her? She could still die and she was thinking about kissing? She gingerly stuck her arms back in her sleeves and buttoned her shirt.

"Here." He extended a bottle of water and she grabbed it and drank greedily.

"Thank you." She tried to give the bottle back.

"Take these." He held two small pills in his palm. "For the pain."

"Thanks." She tossed them in her mouth and swallowed with another sip of water while the soldier started packing up the medical kit. He was cute. In a boyish kind of way. Which seemed a silly description for a large, hard-muscled, military guy. Maybe it was the buzz-cut hair, or his kindness in caring for her.

She shook her head. "How far to the Jeep or helicopter or whatever?"

Zipping up his pack, he slung it over one shoulder, replaced his helmet without snapping the chin straps and stood. He drew in a breath before finally looking at her. "Are you ambulatory?"

She nodded, but before she could straighten, a deep, menacing feline growl echoed somewhere close to them and Gabby froze. She'd grown accustomed to the constant background noises of the jungle. The chirp and buzz of insects, the weird shrieks of birds, the clicks of beetles, even the screeching monkeys, but this—this panther, or leopard, or whatever it was that lived in this jungle, sounded ominous.

Large hands grasped her under the shoulders and lifted her to her feet as if she weighed no more than a feather. She stood face-to-hard-chest with the soldier, so close she could smell a subtle—and pleasant—masculine musk. She became hyper-aware of his hands cupping the sides of her chest. His thumbs rested just above the slope of her breasts. If he slid them down a few inches he could rub the tips of her hardening nipples. Her breathing hitched and she looked up into his eyes.

His Adam's apple moved as his tongue came out to lick his lips. "We gotta go." He removed his hands and stepped back.

Reality intruded on her thoughts. The griminess of her skin. The rough texture of her mud-caked clothes. The ragged tear in the side of her best pencil skirt. And the absurdity of wearing pumps with one heel broken off.

How could she even be thinking about anything sexual right now?

Besides, he hadn't answered her question. "There *is* a Jeep or a helicopter coming for us, right?" she asked.

"Affirmative." Confident. No hesitation. That was good.

He reached into a Velcro-sealed pocket on his pant leg, pulled out a tube of ointment and handed it to her. "This will help with the mosquitoes."

A little late. Bites covered her arms and legs. As she smeared the ointment on exposed skin, he took the bottle of water from her, screwed the lid back on and stuck it in another large pants pocket low on his thigh. "We need to ration this."

Okay, that was less good. "Um…how long—"

"Let's go." He put words into action, sticking his other arm through the backpack strap and hitching it over his shoulder as he strode off.

Tamping down a niggle of dread, Gabby followed. "Look, I realize I kind of lost it back there, but I promise I won't get all hysterical if you tell me the truth. Whatever it is, I can handle knowing bad news better than not knowing."

He stopped and twisted to meet her gaze. "We need to travel about ten clicks—roughly about six miles—by nightfall. I'd rather not travel in the dark."

Panic almost swamped her again, but she drew in a deep breath and let it out slowly. She'd promised not to get hysterical. "Nightfall? We're not...leaving today?"

"The helo will meet us at the extraction location at dawn."

She blinked away irritating tears.

"Look, we need to be moving."

"Right." She nodded.

Facing forward again, he strode away. "If you can't keep up, just let me know, okay?"

"Yes, sir." She hurried to catch up.

"Clay."

Gabby studied the ground but didn't see any. "Where?"

"What?"

"Where's the clay?"

"No, that's my name. Call me Clay, Ms. Diaz."

"Oh!" Even in the heat of this forsaken—no, not forsaken, Abuelita's voice corrected her, God was even in this jungle—Gabby felt her face grow warmer. The soldier must think she was slow-witted. As she had constantly for the past two days, she gripped the medallion on the chain around her neck and asked for faith that they would make it home alive. Abuelita had given her the silver medal for her First Communion and it always comforted her.

"Ms. Diaz?"

The soldier's face came into focus. His concerned face. Because she'd halted.

"We have to keep moving."

"Right." She straightened her shoulders and forced a smile. "Call me Gabby."

CLAY COULDN'T DECIDE if this woman was the bravest civilian he'd ever encountered, or the craziest. Maybe she was both.

For instance, that smile she'd just flashed. After what he'd just told her she should be complaining about something by now. They'd missed the rescue helo. They weren't going to make it to the secondary extraction. And surviving overnight in this jungle was going to prove challenging. But knowing all this, she'd...smiled? And that smile had hit him right in the gut. She'd been held captive, shot at, bitten and scratched up, and wasn't smelling too sweet.

But that hadn't stopped him checking her out. He wasn't called Hounddog for nothing.

Her thin, used-to-be-white shirt was damp and clinging to her, showing through to her very practical, plain white bra. Her dark brown eyes were fringed with thick lashes and didn't miss a thing. And those lips. Made to be thoroughly kissed. Plus she had the kind of figure he loved on a woman. Full and lush in all the right places. He'd had to muster up an extra ounce of discipline wrapping that gauze around her waist.

But he had a job to do.

He heard an abbreviated shriek behind him and spun to check on her.

With a flinch she whisked off a beetle that had landed on her chest. Her lips trembled, but she pinched them together. They'd been traveling about an hour and she was keeping up pretty well, but she looked done in.

Keep her distracted. "So, Gabby." He resumed heading west, hacking through twisting vines and thick fronds with his knife, holding a tangle of ferns out of the way for her. "Where you from?"

"Texas. In the Rio Grande Valley. A little town just outside of Corpus Christi called San Juan."

"And how'd you get into banking?" He glanced back at her.

After seeming confused by his curiosity, she drew in a deep breath. "What can I say, I'm a mathlete. A nerd. Yeah, my Twitter sign is even at symbol nerdy bank analyst. How nerdy is that?"

As he slashed through the dense undergrowth, he listened while she chattered. He could hear the pride in her voice when she talked about going to college. She'd won a scholarship to the University of Corpus Christi, earned a Bachelor of Science in Mathematics and Statistics. Then got her Master of Science in Finance at the U of Texas, San Antonio. Geez, a master's? He'd barely graduated high school. If he hadn't crammed for the ASVAB like a son of a gun, he'd have never passed the Armed Services exam. Book smarts were *not* his strong suit.

"What about you?" She sounded out of breath.

"What *about* me?" She wanted to know if the guy who was saving her butt had a degree?

"Where are *you* from? Somewhere in the South, right?"

Defensive much, Bellamy? "Yes, ma'am. Talladega, Alabama. Home of the Superspeedway and the Peach Jam Jubilee." Would she catch the edge of bitterness to his tone?

"Jubilee? That sounds fun."

Fun? Nothing associated with home sounded fun to him. Except, now that she mentioned it, he guessed maybe he did have a recollection of sitting on his step-dad's shoulders and watching some floats go by. Catching a piece of candy the beautiful Peach Queen threw. Giving the candy to his little sister and her grinning up at him like he was her hero.

And he'd end up playing that role for her over and over again.

"Clay? Is something wrong?"

Wow, that flash of memory brought a tightness to his chest. A distraction he could not afford right now. He cleared his throat. "Not a thing." He checked his diver's watch. Oh-nine-fifty. And they'd only traveled about two clicks. Still, her breathing was labored. The humidity was a factor. And she probably hadn't eaten much, if anything, in the last couple of days. A few feet ahead was a small clearing of sorts. "Let's stop and rest a sec." He sheathed his knife.

As she gave a relieved sigh and moved to sit on a fallen tree branch, he dropped his pack and dug out a protein bar and the water bottle. "Here."

She took them eagerly and he unsnapped his metal flask and allowed himself a mouthful of water, watching the woman for signs of pain, fatigue or mental breakdown.

She was short, but sturdy enough. Other than a wince of pain every so often—probably related to her bullet graze, she seemed in fairly good condition. Her torn skirt showed off her shapely legs. His gaze followed the length of her legs, imagining the rest of her thighs hidden by the skirt. Wondering if her panties matched her plain white bra. For some reason they seemed more erotic than any of that lacy underwear most women he hooked up with wore.

He really was a hound dog.

She tucked her legs under her and folded her arms over her chest, and he met her gaze. Damn. She must feel violated enough already and he'd gone and—but that wasn't anger or fear he saw in her eyes. It was desire.

Which there was no way he was going to act on.

He put away his flask. "We'd better get— Don't move, all right?"

"What?"

"I said, hold completely still."

Though he kept his volume low, she must've responded to the command in his tone because she obeyed. He slid his knife from the holster on his hip, aimed at the long red-black-and-yellow-striped coral snake next to her right foot and threw it with enough force to pin the reptile's head to the ground.

Gabby warily turned her head a fraction and moved just her eyes to glance at the dead snake at her feet.

Her eyes widened. Her mouth dropped open in a silent scream.

Then she started hyperventilating.

3

GABBY COULDN'T BREATHE. Her vision wavered. All the greens ran together around her, and then everything turned black in her peripheral vision.

The next thing she knew, her head was cradled in the crook of Clay's arm and he was stroking her head and murmuring soothing words.

"Just take a deep breath in. That's it, you're gonna be fine."

Gabby opened her eyes. Clay was so close she could see a healthy growth of stubble beneath his dark green face paint. He'd taken off his helmet again, but his sheared hair could've been any color between dark blond to black. With a cowardly whimper she grabbed the front of his shirt and clung to him, pressing her nose into his neck.

She felt his arms tighten around her, aware that he was careful to avoid her bandage. And he rocked her, shushing her, even though she wasn't crying. At that moment she fell just a little bit in love. She wasn't crazy enough to believe the feeling flooding her heart was real. It was just the situation. The shared danger. The heroism of his rescuing her. What woman could resist that? But still… Right now it felt very real.

She reveled in his comfort while at the same time thinking any minute he would push her away and tell her they needed to keep moving. But he didn't. He caressed her shoulder, rubbed her lower back. His shirt was wet from sweat and she wanted to unbutton it and slide her hand beneath to feel his heated skin, feel his strong heartbeat.

Sitting here, cradled in his masculine embrace, she wanted to kiss him. And more. She wanted to make love with him. Right now. Before the next snake, or leopard or kidnapper really did kill her.

But, of course, she wouldn't.

She exhaled, long and cathartic. "Clay?"

"Yeah?" He eased his hold and she raised her head to look into his eyes.

"You're going to get me home, right?"

His eyes narrowed and he smoothed a hand over her snarled hair, fingering a strand away from her face. "You have my word, darlin'."

Darling. She'd never been any man's darling before. Or sweetheart, or any endearment. Of course he didn't mean it that way. It was just a Southern thing. But she still liked him calling her "darlin'."

She wanted to stay like this forever, safe in his embrace, secure in the knowledge that nothing could harm her. He wouldn't let it. But she managed a smile, pushed out of his arms and got to her feet, shaky, but steady enough. "Okay, then." She wiped her palms on her skirt. "We need to keep going, right?"

"Yes, ma'am." He grinned, his eyes crinkling at the corners as he retrieved his knife, reached for his backpack and helmet, and rose in one fluid motion. His smile spoke to her and squeezed her heart.

Snapping his helmet onto his backpack, he led the way, storming forward through the thick vegetation, hacking at vines with his huge serrated knife and glancing back to check on her every once in a while.

She'd give him the thumbs-up and a smile, and concentrate on not falling behind. Her wrecked shoes chafed the backs of her heels, and what parts of her weren't covered in mud were covered in mosquito bites. But at least they seemed to be heading downhill. Unfortunately, the farther they traveled down the mountain, the hotter it got.

The heat was suffocating; the air so thick, each breath she drew was like drinking. She'd lived through many a blistering summer in South Texas. But none could compare to the humidity of this jungle.

Still, they trekked on for what seemed like hours.

"Want some more water?" Clay's concerned tone must mean she'd started to lag behind.

She picked up her pace. "No, I'm good." Despite her thirst, she'd had to…go for a long time now.

Sitting in that hole with James for all day and night, she'd quickly given up any expectations of privacy and did what she'd needed to. James had been oblivious to anything except his own fears and discomforts, anyway.

But this was Clay.

Plus…snakes.

"Well, I could use a rest." He stopped and pulled out the bottle of water from his pants pocket and handed it to her.

He wasn't even breathing hard, so she highly doubted he was tired, but he produced a flat, plastic canteen from another pocket, and took a small sip.

This was horrifying and ridiculous at the same time. In a minute she'd have to cross her legs. She might as well get the humiliation over with and admit her dilemma. "Um, I have to…"

He blinked at her. Then his eyes widened. "Oh! Yeah. Sure. Me, too." His expression reverted to soldier-on-a-mission. "I'll take the north, you take the south." With a nod of his head he indicated to his right, then his left. She hadn't seen him check a compass, so how could he possibly know which way was north?

Even as he disappeared into the vegetation to their right, she stood frozen. The crunching of leaves beneath his feet silenced. But even in the stillness, insects buzzed and birds called. Monkeys chattered. What if he was attacked by an animal or bit by a snake? What if he didn't come back? Irrational fear seized her. No way could she tramp off into the dense jungle forest alone, no matter how badly she needed to—

"All done?"

Gabby snapped her head toward Clay. "I don't think I can."

His gaze drifted away and his jaw muscle ticked. The green face paint was wearing off in patches where he'd wiped at sweat. A shaft of sunlight hit his cheek as he stepped forward. "Sure you can." He took her arm and propelled her a few feet into the undergrowth. "I'll be right here. You go ahead, now." Putting a thin tree between them, he spun on his boot heel and folded his arms, staring off into the distance.

But Clay's close proximity caused a different dilemma. He might not be able to see her with his back turned, but he would still be able to *hear* her. Maybe the deafening sounds of nature would drown her out.

But…snakes.

"Um, Clay?"

"Yeah?"

"Can I borrow your knife?"

No answer. Maybe he didn't trust her with a dangerous weapon. Then he unsnapped the leather holster at his hip and pulled out the wicked-looking knife, flipped it, caught it by the blade and extended the handle toward her.

She swallowed and took it. "Thank you." Only then did she realize what needed doing actually required two free hands. After dithering a moment, she stuck the handle of the knife between her teeth, thoroughly checked the ground for anything slithering nearby and then got on with it.

When she approached him, he handed her the water bottle without a word and she returned his knife and rinsed her hands, and they headed back to the makeshift path he'd been cutting for them. A wave of exhaustion overcame her when she thought about continuing on. Her back stung. She was hot, and sticky, and her feet burned where the heels chafed, and— "Listen to yourself, you whiny baby! At least you're alive."

Clay was waiting for her, watching her with a wary expression. She realized she'd spoken out loud. Great, now he'd think she was bonkers. She knew she tended to talk to herself a lot. Most of the time, it didn't matter.

"You good to go?" He was waiting for her, so she smiled and nodded, and trudged on.

She lost all sense of time as the day wore on. She thought about being home in San Juan, how glad her parents would be to see her again. About Jorge, and Bernard, and Patricia. She missed them. And she fingered her Mary medal as she prayed to her Abuelita. She couldn't wait to see Mama and Papa. Finally, twilight settled over the tall trees. Clay hadn't said a word. Even when he occasionally handed her the water bottle. "By tomorrow I'll have a cool shower and clean clothes." *One foot in front of the other.* "And I'm going to brush my teeth twice, and wash my hair three times and buy a new—"

Clay spun and clamped a hand over her mouth.

CLAY HELD A finger in front of his lips. He'd heard voices at three o'clock, speaking in what he thought must be Guarani, a native language of Paraguay. That, by itself, didn't mean much. Over 80 percent of Paraguayans spoke Guarani. And he'd only been able to catch a few words. But one of them had been a Spanish word thrown in: *Americano.*

They were going to have to double back. He hoped not very far or they risked missing the helo. Then he recognized what else he heard in the distance. The roar of rushing water. They were closer to the Rio Bermejo than he'd thought. Thanks to Gabby's fortitude, they'd made good time. Even if she had talked for most of the afternoon. He didn't think she was even aware she'd been talking out loud. And the crazy thing was, he hadn't minded. He'd liked listening to her voice, liked hearing about her close-knit family.

Mentally going over the map he'd studied on the plane ride down, he guesstimated the distance to the river. If they could travel by water tonight—depending on the current—they could make up the time they'd lose doubling back. He just really hadn't wanted to travel at night. Lighting their way might as well shine a big bull's-eye on their position.

But before he could worry about that, they had to avoid detection by the men who'd been asking about the *Americanos*. Slowly, he lifted his hand off Gabby's mouth, slid his Sig from its shoulder holster and signaled to Gabby to stay put while he investigated the possible unfriendly's position.

Careful to step light and move slow, Clay inched up to the edge of the clearing. He took up position behind a tree, pulled out his binoculars and spied a farmer in his wide-brimmed hat leading an ox away from the creek. No sign of anyone else. He scanned the meadow, but daylight was fading fast. Then, on the edge of his vision he caught a shadow. Two shadows. He lifted the binoculars again. They were armed. And they were headed this way.

When he returned to Gabby she was standing exactly where he'd left her, still, and as frightened as a deer in headlights. But she wasn't panicking. And she'd obeyed his order. Which he hadn't been sure he could count on.

Knowing how sound could carry, he spoke low in her ear. "We're turning around. Follow the path I cleared, move quickly, but try to step softly. All right?"

Her breathing was shallow, but she nodded and did as he asked. Clay followed behind her trying to cover their tracks as best he could. He hadn't disturbed the vegetation at the edge of the meadow. With any luck, the hunters wouldn't find their trail.

They'd traveled only ten minutes before darkness swallowed the forest and he was forced to click on his pin light. He covered the top and shone it only on the jungle floor, but he still felt like he might as well have gift wrapped their position to the kidnappers. His gut clenched as he heard leaves rustling behind them.

He clicked off the light, grabbed Gabby and pulled her off the path. Hand over her mouth again, he held her still and waited.

Frogs croaked. Crickets chirped. A pygmy owl hooted.

The rustling drew closer. The kidnappers were practically on top of them, the shafts of light from their flashlights barely missing them. Gabby tensed and tightened her arms around his waist. He didn't know when they'd put their arms around each other, but he lowered his head close to hers and stroked her hair. He still held his Sig in the other hand down by his side, slowed his breathing and prepared to spin and shoot.

The bandits walked right past them. The sounds of their crunching footsteps faded.

Clay became aware of her breathing, her soft breasts pressed against his chest. She lifted her face and her lips brushed his with a quick intake of breath.

He didn't move, letting his mouth hover over hers. She let out the softest moan. She was so small, petite, the top of her head barely reached his shoulders, but her body was full and lush, her stomach cushioning his growing hard-on.

His blood pounding, his pulse racing, he wanted to take her trembling lips with his so badly.

Don't do it.

He dropped his hands and stepped back. Closing his eyes, he drew in a deep, clearing breath. His mission was hostage rescue. That should be his only thought. Getting Gabby out of Paraguay safe and sound. Not how he wanted to pull her to him and kiss her. And certainly not how he wished he could cup her breasts in his palms, slide his hand—

Right, Bellamy. Get your head in the game. She was his responsibility.

He had to get control of himself and figure out what their next move would be. But, now that the immediate danger had passed, all he could think about was how she'd felt in his arms, how her quiet little moan had made his body come alive.

"Are they— Are they gone?" she whispered.

Snapping back to the here and now, he focused on the sounds of the jungle around them. "Long gone. We're safe for now." He holstered the Sig while he ran through various scenarios in his head. Night had shrouded the jungle in darkness. He had his night vision goggles, but Gabby would be left trailing after him essentially blind. And he couldn't risk lighting their way again. No choice now. "We'll hunker down here for the night, and then make our way to the extraction point at first light."

That decided, he slid out his knife, slipped the goggles down over his eyes and cut several large, smooth palm fronds to build a makeshift cover. Chances were it'd be misting, if not outright raining before dawn.

He whispered for Gabby to join him under the leafy umbrella, but she didn't move. "You checked for snakes?"

He smiled as he flipped the goggles onto the top of his head. "All clear."

With a brief flash of white teeth, she sat beside him and he retrieved his MRE from his pack and offered it to her. "Dinner is served, ma'am."

He could tell she was trying not to grab it from him and devour every bite. "Don't you want some?"

"Not really hungry." He pushed the ready meal into her hand.

Ignoring his growling stomach, he sipped the last of his water. They'd be at the river by oh-seven-hundred. And back at forward base by lunch. He'd gone way longer than this without eating. Even *before* he joined the military.

After hesitating a moment, she shrugged and finished off the food in minutes along with most of her water, then borrowed his knife again, along with his night vision goggles, and disappeared a couple of yards away. When she needed to return he called softly so she could sound her way back.

She dropped down next to him, returned his goggles and then scooted closer, leaning on his arm. "How far to the rescue site?"

"Less than a mile, I'd say. I'll wake you when it's time to go." He slipped the strap of the goggles over his head and scanned the area.

"Do you think they'll come back?"

"Doubtful. They won't want to travel far in this jungle at night any more than we do."

"Still…"

When she didn't finish her thought, he asked, "What?"

"Do you have an extra gun?"

He did, but he wasn't about to give it to her. "You had any training with a weapon?"

"No, but—"

"Tell you what. There are a few basic moves that'll get you out of any hold."

"Oh, like self-defense stuff?"

"Yeah, I could teach you a couple, all right?"

"Okay. I *should* know how to defend myself. That was one of the things I thought of the last couple of da—ys." A huge yawn interrupted the end of her sentence and her head landed on his shoulder.

"You should get some rest."

"You promise you'll teach me those moves?"

Clay smiled. The last couple of words had been mumbled. He'd bet she was barely awake. "I promise." If they had time, he would. "Now try to sleep."

There was silence for a moment before she raised her head. "Aren't you sleeping, too?"

"I'm going to keep watch for a while."

He heard her exhale a large sigh, and then lowered her head back onto his shoulder. "Okay, good night."

After less than a minute her head drooped forward, and he slipped his arm around her as she slumped into his lap.

Clay tried to ignore her soft body pressing into him. He listened past the bird calls and chirping insects for any man-made sounds, and scanned the area continuously while his charge slept the sleep of the exhausted, mumbling, at times moaning, or sighing. She wasn't a quiet sleeper either.

After another moan she turned and nuzzled into his stomach. Great. His body had a will of its own when it came to a woman's mouth being that close to his cock. His pants got uncomfortable and he tried to slowly shift their positions.

"What?" She lifted her head, the whites of her eyes blinking up at him. She sat up, pushing off his thigh with her hand. Her palm cupped his rock-hard erection. But instead of moving her hand away, she stilled. Several beats passed, yet he allowed her hand to stay where it was. She slowly began to trace his cock up to its root and back down to the tip again.

He bit off a strangled sound. Before he could stop her she cupped his face in her palms and fit her lips to his, at the same time she rose up and straddled his thigh. He pressed her close, all the while his brain was shouting for him to get control. When she rubbed her hot center against him, he got even harder. He hadn't thought that could be possible. He felt her fingers run over the short hair at the back of his head and he gave in, returning her kiss, coaching her to open to him, deepening it.

Her lips were as full and lush as her body. He cupped and squeezed her butt, and she hummed her approval. He lost himself so much that, when she would've pulled away, he followed and lingered, teasing her with his tongue. He wanted more.

She was kissing him for all she was worth, and he was letting her. His mind was thinking any minute now he'd stop. He shouldn't do this. But his mouth moved over hers with the hunger of a teenage boy.

When she finally came up for air, she was still clinging to his face, stroking his temples. "Make love to me, Clay."

4

EVEN IN THE PITCH-DARK, Gabby could tell she'd made a huge mistake.

Clay froze for an instant, then set her off his lap and sprang to his feet. "I need to check the perimeter," he said tonelessly. His shadow moved silently away.

Her face flamed and she closed her eyes. She couldn't believe she'd done that.

But she refused to regret it. She shoved her thick, tangled hair away from her face. She'd been kidnapped, thrown into a hole in the ground, shot at and almost bitten by a deadly snake. And she wasn't safe yet.

What about all the things she'd never done? All the risks she'd never taken, the chances that might have been lost forever. All her life she'd let fear prevent her from truly living. And fear of what? Of making a fool of herself? She'd survive that. Clay *had* returned her kiss. And that hard length beneath her palm had *not* been his gun. Her thighs clenched in need just thinking about the feel of him beneath her hand. Remembering his mouth moving over hers, his tongue, his hands caressing down her hips…

Was she going to worry about disappointing her parents? That, too, seemed so irrelevant now. What if she died without having really lived?

She clasped her Mary medal. She was done worrying about what other people thought. Done being the good girl. From now on she was going to live life to the fullest. Take risks. Go for it.

Resolve swept over her, winding its way through her psyche, obliterating her embarrassment.

"You awake?" As quietly as he'd left, Clay returned, giving her a verbal warning in his soft Southern drawl before he crouched beside her.

"Yes." She definitely wasn't going back to sleep anytime soon.

An awkward silence passed. One thing she did regret was that her actions had made him feel uncomfortable. "Look, I'm sorry, I—"

"No. I get it. You've been through a lot. It's the whole 'Speed' thing, right? Shared danger can produce intense feelings of intimacy. But that doesn't mean they're real feelings."

"No." She fiddled with the collar of her blouse, pulling the ends together. "That's not it."

"Believe me. Situations like this—it's pretty normal."

"No, you don't understand." Through the dark she found the shadow where she thought his face was. "I could've died. *Still* could. And there's so much I've never done. Never experienced. And I don't want to die

without knowing what it's like to…to *be* with someone."

The sound of chirping crickets in the face of Clay's
silence would've struck her as comical if she wasn't
so mortified. She wished she could at least see his expression. Did he get what she was saying? Did he understand?

Growing up, she'd been taught sex was something
sacred between a husband and a wife. That her body
was something she needed to respect and save for marriage. And even if she had been tempted as she got
older, her average looks and nerdy shyness had kept
the big decision out of her hands.

Once she reached college she hadn't remained a virgin out of some sense of morality or even inhibition.
She'd come close a couple of times. But the longer she
waited, the more important it seemed that it should be
with the right guy. And so far…the right guy had never
turned up. Until now.

"You've never…?" Clay sounded incredulous. Of
course he was shocked that any twenty-six-year-old
would still be a virgin. And worse, he was horrified. As
if he thought she still wanted him to…accommodate her.

Gabby pressed her palms to her eyes. Why had she
told him? Why had she felt the need to explain? If only
she had just kept quiet, and let the moment pass. She
uncovered her eyes. "Oh, please can we just forget the
whole thing?"

After another long moment, she felt him shift to
a sitting position, caught an impression of his arms

hanging off his knees. "Got about two, maybe three hours till dawn."

Thank goodness he wasn't any more anxious to pursue the subject than she was.

She nodded. He probably couldn't see her, but his announcement hadn't really required an answer.

More silence.

Could she take three to four hours of sitting here, wondering what he was thinking of her? Worrying about snakes, and kidnappers, and imagining all the many scenarios where they didn't make it out of here alive? She'd lose it for sure. She needed a distraction. Like a bolt, an idea hit her. "Hey, you never told me about the Peach Jam Jubilee."

CLAY GRIMACED. As a change of topic, it sucked, but at least they weren't talking about feelings and—he cringed. People who'd never had sex before.

For a virgin she was an awfully good kisser. Too good. Trouble was, he'd been so into that kiss he'd forgotten all about his job. His duty. And that was unacceptable. Not during a mission. Not ever. No woman had ever distracted him like that. And no woman ever would.

"Clay?"

"Yeah." He cleared his throat. "What is there to tell? It's just your usual hometown parade. The Peach Queen gets crowned and waves at everybody from her float."

"Sounds...peachy." She snickered.

Clay couldn't stop a smile. She was something else.

Cracking jokes after all she'd been through. "Yeah. There's peach jam, peach pie, peach preserves."

"Peach cobbler." She gasped. "Peach ice cream," she moaned the words.

That throaty, feminine sound made his breath catch. *Don't go there.* "And don't forget peachy pork chops."

"Pork chops?"

"You've never had 'em? They're good."

She groaned. "Now you're making me really hungry."

She didn't know the half of it. He snapped his night vision goggles down over his eyes and scanned the area. "You should try to get some shut-eye." This time he'd be prepared for all those sexy little noises she made in her sleep. And the feel of her body against his.

"I don't think I can."

She wiggled and bumped into him and he looked over. She was clutching a silver medal hanging around her neck and biting her lip. Her skirt was hitched up to midthigh. She had beautiful legs. Her hips were curvy, but her waist was small. And that thin white shirt outlined her beautiful— He flipped the goggles up. Didn't seem fair that he could see her and she couldn't see him.

"What about the—the Speedway? Do you like car racing?"

He shrugged. "It's okay. I went a few times in high school.

"What else did you do growing up in Talladega?"

Seriously? He'd rather go through BUD/S training all over again than talk about his life before the Navy. "Not much."

The woman stayed quiet so long he knew—*he just knew*—she was staring at him expectantly. What? She wanted him to spill his life story? *Not gonna happen.* "It was just a regular town, with regular people, okay?"

"Okay." She sounded disappointed. "So, you're like a Special Forces kind of guy in the military? What is that, a Marine?"

He scoffed and threw her an insulted glare she probably couldn't see. "I'm a US Navy SEAL."

"Oooo, wow. A SEAL? Like the guys that got Bin Laden? Were you there?"

He shook his head. "That was SEAL Team 6."

"What's the difference? I mean, do all the teams have different specialties?"

"Some. SEAL Team 6 focuses more on counterterrorism. We're SEAL Team 2. Artic Warfare, Rescue Ops."

"Well, thank you for coming after me—us."

"That's my job."

"Right, of course."

Clay sighed. That hadn't come out right. She'd been a real trooper, considering they'd traipsed through the jungle all day in sweltering conditions, and she'd almost been bitten by a venomous coral snake. She was just trying to make it through the night. Seemed the least he could do was talk to her.

Besides, after tomorrow, he'd never see her again. She'd asked about growing up in Talladega? He quietly sighed. "So, no Peach Jam Jubilee where you're from?"

"In Texas?" She sounded insulted, but in a good-natured way. He caught her white teeth in the darkness. "It's all football, all the time. My two brothers live and breathe the game. Did you play?"

"No, but my sister was a cheerleader."

"Does she still live in Talladega?"

"Yep. I'm the only one that got out."

"Got out? You didn't like it there?"

He ground his back teeth. "Just nothing for me there. More opportunities elsewhere."

She made a nodding-in-agreement type sound. "That's why I moved to New York. I want to help my parents. They work so hard." He could hear the genuine love in her voice and it bothered him.

"My papa is the grounds custodian for a famous shrine in San Juan. My mama cleans houses. I was the first one in my family to graduate high school."

Clay was pretty sure his mom and stepfather hadn't graduated high school either. Even Ashley almost hadn't. And he'd left for basic training before his own graduation ceremony. No walking across the stage to get his diploma or throw his cap in the air. It's not like his parents would've gone, anyway.

"What do *your* parents do?"

He snapped shut his memories. "They both work at the quarry."

"Quarry? I didn't know Alabama had a quarry."

"More than one. Probably the largest industry in the state. If I hadn't joined the Navy I'd probably still be working there."

"You worked there, too? Like, actually digging out the rocks?"

"Yep."

"What kind of stone?"

"Marble, mostly. Some limestone, and a few other minerals, but Alabama's famous for its white marble."

"Huh."

"Started when I was fourteen. Lied about my age to get the job, too, if you can believe that. It was back-breaking work. Other than my paycheck every two weeks, I hated everything about it."

She made a sympathetic sound and he squeezed his eyes closed. How had they switched to talking about *his* life again? "Tell me about New York."

She made a different sound this time, a hum somewhere between excitement and nervousness. "Manhattan is so different from my little hometown. Growing up I never would've thought I'd live there. I have a little studio apartment in Greenwich Village. It's small, but I love it. There's a library right across the street and on the weekends, I love to take my laptop and just hang out there."

"At the library? You live in one of the most exciting cities in the world. Don't you want to party on the weekends?"

"I'm not really the partying type." Her voice lowered. "I told you I was a nerd. Hanging out at the library is about the most exciting thing nerds do."

He could kick himself for bringing that self-doubt into her voice. "You sure don't look like a nerd."

Funny how he could sense her stillness. He winced. He hadn't meant to use his pickup-line tone. He wasn't at Barney's on a Friday night trying to find some hot woman.

Reaching into his pocket, he pulled out the other protein bar he'd been saving for her and held it out in front of her. "Here."

"What is it?"

"Breakfast."

"Oh." When she groped for the bar her fingers grazed the back of his hand and he had the crazy urge to grab her hand and bring it to his lips. Dawn couldn't come soon enough.

"Thank you."

"No problem."

He heard the crinkling of the wrapper. "You want half?"

"I have another. You eat that one."

Out of nowhere rain began pelting down. Good. He needed to cool off. He pushed to his feet. "Gonna check the area again. Try to sleep. When I get back, we'll head out."

5

IN SOME WAYS, her time in the Paraguayan jungle seemed
like a dream.

Well, more like a nightmare.

Except for the last night.

Chin propped on her palm, Gabby stared at the report
on her computer screen. Her supervisor wanted this data
analysis done as soon as possible, but she'd been staring
at the same column of numbers for more than half an
hour. Which was not a good sign for her first day back.

But her mind kept drifting. Remembering…

How she'd had to squint at the bright sun reflecting
off the river as she and Clay broke through the dense
foliage that morning. How the water had sprayed a fine
mist on her face as a thunderous helicopter chopped

through the air. How Clay's hand clapping her shoulder had reassured her as he snapped a harness around her chest and then gave the thumbs-up signal to the men waiting to haul her up.

Clay.

Once the helicopter landed at the embassy, a nurse had tried to whisk her away before she could tell him goodbye. He'd been talking to one of the other soldiers and hadn't even glanced in her direction.

All she could think was that she'd never see him again.

Setting her jaw, she'd wrenched from the nurse, ran to him and thrown her arms around him. He'd held his arms out away from his sides as if he had no idea how to handle such a display of emotion. But despite his stiff reserve, she'd buried her nose in his strong chest, and then looked up into light brown eyes that glinted with wariness.

She'd dropped her arms and stepped back from him with a smile, trying not to burst into tears. "You were phenomenal."

"Just a grunt doing his job, ma'am," he'd said with a solemn nod.

He'd been so much more to her. But she hadn't said that. "Well. Thank you, anyway."

He'd nodded again. "You take care, now." Then he'd turned and strode away, back to the helicopter. She'd watched as he climbed in and the chopper lifted off and flew away.

He hadn't looked back.

"How is it being back at work?" James appeared at her cubicle.

Gabby jumped, her heart racing. "James," she gulped his name. "You scared me."

He frowned, looking hurt and concerned at the same time. "I'm sorry."

"No, no. It's not your fault. I'm jumpy lately."

"Me, too. Ever since…" He gestured vaguely to the room. "You know."

Gabby nodded. At her boss's insistence, she'd spent two weeks recovering with her parents in Texas before New York Corporate Bank Inc. allowed her to return to work. But the time off hadn't really helped. She still had nightmares. Insomnia. Depression.

Her family was worried, but they didn't understand. Didn't know what to do for her, or how to act. She'd found herself resenting their normalcy. Their ability to go about their everyday lives while she—she kept seeing Mr. V with blood gushing out of his head.

She'd been told they'd recovered his body. There was a funeral in New York, but Gabby had still been in Texas. Half of her had wanted to attend the service. The other half had worried that she would completely lose it and embarrass herself. She just couldn't believe he was dead. Gone forever.

And she'd come so close to meeting the same end.

James stepped into her cubicle and drummed his fingers on her desk. "It might help to talk about it. Want to get some lunch?"

No, she didn't. "I brought mine from home." She pointed at the brown paper bag sitting beside the print-out of reports she'd planned to work on while she ate. "I'm weeks behind."

"Yeah, sure. I understand." James stuck his hands in his pockets and stared at the floor. "I just wanted to apologize for the way I acted. Before we were rescued, I mean." He winced and raised devastated eyes to hers.

"It's okay." She reached up and patted his upper arm. "It was a horrible ordeal. And no one really knows how they'll react under such circumstances."

Except, a small voice crept into her thoughts, *Clay would never have acted that way.* He had protected her, reassured her and, ultimately, saved them. Of course, he was a soldier. He'd been trained to handle unspeakable violence and mind-numbing terror. But even so, there'd been something about the man. An indefinable quality that no training could give.

"I can't sleep," James said quietly. "And when I do sleep I have nightmares."

"Me, too, sometimes."

"The counselor says it's PTSD."

She nodded. James did look thinner. Haggard, with dark circles under his eyes. Did she look as bad? What had happened to her resolve that night in the jungle to take risks and live life to the fullest? Back in the real world, it wasn't so easy.

James was still staring at the floor, picking at a fingernail. "Do you feel like sometimes everyone is looking at you? And like you just want to scream at them?"

"Yes." She hadn't meant to say that out loud. But finally, someone who understood. If she was to get back some semblance of a normal life she had to start somewhere, right? She got to her feet and stuck her lunch sack in her file cabinet drawer. "I changed my mind. Let's grab some hot dogs and eat at the park."

James's head snapped up and he smiled. "That'd be great."

SHE BEGAN EATING lunch with James almost every day, and talking with him did help. Despite his pitiable behavior during the kidnapping, he understood what she was feeling. She could tell him things.

They'd experienced this horrible ordeal together, and with James she was able to work through her complicated feelings. She was angry, but appreciated being alive. She wanted to curl up and be alone, but she also wanted to go running through the streets screaming. She yearned for someone special in her life. But the only person she thought about all the time was a complete stranger who just happened to be assigned to rescue her.

Of course she didn't mention that last part to James.

"I notice you rub your necklace a lot," he said while they were having their usual lunch in the park the following week. He motioned to the silver charm around her neck.

"It's a medal. The Miraculous Medal of the Virgin Mary. My Abuelita—my grandmother—gave it to me for my First Communion. I've worn it ever since."

"It must be very special."

"She died not long after. I kind of think of her as my guardian angel. The medal has always made me feel safe."

He smiled, stood and leaned over the table to finger it, studying it closely.

Gabby stiffened. He was too close. His cologne, always overapplied, was especially cloying this close.

Finally, he let go and returned to his seat, eyeing her with a meaningful glimmer.

She looked away. What was the matter with her? Just because he wasn't Clay...

Pigeons were pecking at crumbs on the ground around her. Zuccotti Park was nice in the spring. A brisk mid-March breeze made her lunch sack flutter, and she could see a few bright green leaf buds trying to catch some of the sun's rays on the tree limbs above her. Soon, it would be Easter.

Last year on Palm Sunday hundreds of local Catholics had processed down Broadway, passing right by here, carrying palm fronds and singing "Hosanna" on their way to Mass. She'd wanted to join them, but she had talked herself out of going, too timid. Now, her reasons—that she wouldn't know anyone, that it would be crowded and intimidating—seemed weak and, like so many other excuses she had for not doing anything remotely exciting, irrelevant.

"So, you want to go see a movie or something tonight?"

Gabby looked up from her sandwich. A movie. Sitting in a dark theater alone with James? Like a date? He'd become a good friend but...she didn't think she could ever feel *that* way about him.

Wait. Was she just making excuses again? Was it a habit so ingrained that she would never be able to break free from her self-defeating mentality? What was the worst thing that could happen? It wasn't as if she was promising to be his girlfriend. It was one date. She could just go for it. See how she felt afterward. Her braver self— the one from the jungle—would've said *yes*, wouldn't she?

"Never mind." James tossed the remains of his lunch in the trash can. "It was a bad idea."

"Wait." She smiled at him. "I'd love to go."

"Yeah?" James smiled so big she could see his gums. "Sure."

"Text me your address and I'll pick you up."

Gabby hesitated. If she was going to be braver, live more, then she needed to really step out of her comfort zone, take risks. And she hadn't made chicken mole since Christmas. Her mouth watered at the thought of the chili and chocolate sauce. And she should have a guy over to her apartment. Even if it was just for a meal. "Come about six and I'll make something for dinner."

"Sounds great." He moved his hand to cover hers on the table between them.

Her instinct was to snatch it away. But why? Maybe she just couldn't get past the way he'd acted during the kidnapping. And that wasn't really fair to him. So she forced herself to keep her hand in his.

When he rubbed his thumb over her knuckles, she looked up and met his gaze. His smile was so... possessive. And she saw two things in his eyes she wished she didn't see. Desire. And something even worse.

Hope.

THE TALL BRUNETTE in the middle booth smiled at him. Frog hog alert. He'd seen her and her friends at Barney's before, flirting outrageously with other SEALs—aka frogmen—and leaving with them. Just what he was looking for.

Clay broke the triangle of balls on the pool table and then returned her smile. She was leggy and tanned, with pretty hazel eyes and a wide mouth. Dressed kind of skimpy for March, but then, this was Barney's Pool Hall, not the Kennedy Center. He should head over there, buy her a drink and take her out on the dance floor for a little two-stepping. Then see if she wanted to get out of here.

While he waited for a good country song to play, he studied the pool table for possible shots and tried to examine why he wasn't already over there offering to buy her a beer. Well, he *had* just started this game. And she was talking with her girlfriend now, anyway. If she wasn't still sitting there when he finished sinking the solids, no big deal.

No big deal? He hadn't gone home with a woman in almost a month. Not since before... Paraguay.

Gabby. He never should've kissed her.

He pictured her the last time he'd seen her. Her long black hair falling in a tangled mess down her back. Filthy, limping, resolute. Running back to hug him. Telling him he was phenomenal. Like he was some kind of hero. When she'd been the truly brave one. Smiling in the face of overwhelming danger.

Smart and brave. Not his type at all. In fact, just the opposite. She practically screamed white picket fence.

Hell, she was a virgin. But he did wonder how she was doing after such an ordeal. Curiosity about someone he'd rescued was normal, right?

Just for laughs, he pulled out his phone and checked out her Twitter page. @nerdybank-something?

Searching brought it up quickly.

#bankingpunoftheday Mathematicians are often reluctant to cosine a loan.

He didn't get it. He checked the definition of the word *cosine*.

Okay, that didn't help at all. She was a true brainiac. Definitely out of his league.

His thumb hovered over the follow button several seconds...and then he clicked it. Didn't hurt to learn new words, did it? He was just curious.

He checked out another of her Tweets.

@nerdybankanalyst
Learning to cope with nightmares. Talking with friends helps. Looking forward to getting back to normal. #PTSDnotfun

Clay frowned. She was having nightmares? He knew guys who'd come back from a mission and then had some sleepless nights. He'd had a few himself. *That* they could have a conversation about.

What? What was he doing? He wasn't going to have a conversation with her. He didn't even know the woman. Well, he knew she had sweet lips and a shy smile. He knew she had a loving family and a rare kind of courage in a person her age.

Still, he needed to shake off his memories of her. Concentrate on what was right in front of him. He glanced at the brunette.

Just as soon as he finished this game. He bent over, took a shot and sunk one of the solids. As he straightened, he realized the brunette had moved right behind him.

"Playing all by yourself?" She cocked a hip against the pool table and brushed her hand through her hair, giving him a sultry smile.

Too easy.

He wouldn't be anything special to her. Just another SEAL she could say she'd had. What was he thinking? Did that matter? Sex was sex. But how many beds had he gotten up out of in the morning and still felt… unsatisfied? He just wanted more tonight. A fuller, curvier figure. A smile that spoke volumes. Big, dark eyes that looked up at him as if he rocked her world and said if she couldn't have him, then no one else would do.

The brunette's smile had faded. She was about to turn away. What was he *doing*? He had to get out of this rut.

He stepped forward and put his hand at her waist. "Hey, sorry, I was somewhere else for a sec. How about I buy you a drink?"

Her smile returned. "That would be great."

"Don't believe a word he says, ma'am."

Clay would know that voice anywhere. He turned, and his buddy Neil stood there with his arms crossed over his chest. Clay still hadn't gotten used to seeing him in civilian clothes.

He clasped Neil's right hand in a hard shake and pulled him in for a quick slap on the shoulder. "Barrow, you Goody Two-shoes."

"Bellamy, you dumb hick," Neil growled, and then grinned.

Neil was the one person on earth who could get away with calling Clay dumb. And that was only because Clay knew Neil didn't mean it. He let out a heavy sigh. "I suppose I have to buy you a beer now." Clay caught the waitress's eye and held up two fingers.

"And I suppose I have to beat you at pool."

"You can surely try."

Neil's gaze cut over to the brunette still waiting beside Clay. "I think I interrupted…"

Clay spared a glance at the girl, who'd raised an exasperated brow. He could at least relieve her of her phone number, but… "How about a rain check, darlin'."

"In your dreams." She huffed off.

Neil shook his head and tsked. "It's a sad day when Hounddog loses his touch with the ladies."

Clay shrugged. Still, when the waitress brought their beers, Clay had a pitcher of margaritas sent over to the brunette's booth.

"To the ladies." Clay extended his brown bottle to Neil's for a toast.

"To my special lady," Neil retorted as he clinked his bottle to Clay's.

Clay grimaced. "Talk about losing your touch. Piper's got you on a tight leash these days."

Neil grinned. "One man's leash is another man's anchor."

"Exactly." Poor sucker.

"I meant that she keeps me grounded—never mind. How about my safe harbor?"

Clay scoffed.

"I'm happy, Clay. Don't knock it until you've tried it, my friend."

"That'll be the day." Why did men fall for the happily ever after fantasy? Just about every SEAL he knew had been divorced, but it seemed like they always went back for more. At least Neil hadn't actually married Piper.

"Speaking of my special lady, I have a favor to ask."

"Flying to India to help you rescue her brother wasn't enough?"

"Help me rescue?" Neil raised a brow.

"Well, practically."

"Whatever. This is way more dangerous."

"If it's dangerous, I'm there for you." What had his buddy gotten himself into now? Neil's new security firm dealt mostly with providing bodyguards to celebrities. Didn't seem like that should be such a scary gig. "What's going on?"

Neil's jaw tightened. He looked deadly serious. "I want you to be my best man."

Clay stood frozen for a moment. Stunned. The ink was barely dry on Neil's divorce papers. And what a disaster *that* marriage had been. It'd turned out Neil's ex had been threatening Piper and had caused such a stink for him professionally he'd almost been court-martialed. As it was, Neil had been forced to resign from the Navy. And now he wanted to marry again? Was he just a glutton for punishment? "What'd you do, knock her up?"

Neil yanked Clay by his T-shirt and shook him. His eyes narrowed with barely restrained violence. "You don't ever disrespect Piper, you hear me?"

What the—? Neil would fight him? Over a female? "Okay, okay." Clay held his hands up in surrender. "I apologize, all right?"

Neil's menacing expression cleared as he let him go. "You're lucky we've been friends for so long."

Clay had to take a deep breath to calm his temper. The unexpected assault had zapped him back in time to one of his earliest memories. His stepdad walloping him so hard he'd fallen back and slammed into a table. He'd told Clay that he'd upset his mama and warned that he better learn his manners or he'd get a real whoopin'.

To this day Clay had no idea what he'd done.

Now, he tugged his T-shirt down, smoothed out the wrinkles. Neil was right about one thing. They'd been friends for too long to let anyone or anything come between them. "If you still want me, I'd be honored."

Neil grinned and clapped him on the shoulder. "Can't imagine getting married without you there."

"Listen, Neil. No disrespect, but—are you sure?"

Neil's face took on a seriously love-struck look. "I'm surer than I've ever been about anything. And if you're very lucky, someday you'll understand."

Lucky? Like his mother had been lucky? Married to

a bully for twenty-plus years? Or like most of his SEAL buddies? Cheated on, or coming home from deployments to find their wives had left them, and seeing their kids every other weekend? But Clay kept his thoughts to himself. "So, when's this happening?"

"Not until the fall. You know how women are. Piper wants the whole white dress scenario."

Clay nodded and took a swallow of his beer. *Did* he know how women were? Oh yeah, he knew.

"Hey, I wanted to ask you something else."

"Don't worry, there'll be a stripper at your bachelor party."

"Um, not sure Piper would appreciate that, but that's not it." He turned and grabbed a cue stick and examined the tip. "I want you to come join my firm." Finally, he met Clay's gaze. "Your days of going on ops are limited. You could retire, move to Florida—"

"Thanks, but no thanks."

"What are you going to do when you can't deploy anymore? Tell me your body doesn't complain after every mission."

Clay shook his head. "I just can't see myself as a bodyguard to the rich and famous, man."

Neil's mouth flattened.

Great. He'd just insulted his best bud. "Hey, I didn't mean it like that. I know what you do is important. I just...don't think civilian life is for me."

"Well, if you change your mind, I sure could use you." Neil sipped his beer and studied the game already in play. "I'll take stripes. Loser buys the next round."

"You're on." Clay chalked his cue, but his mind wasn't on the game.

What *was* he going to do when he could no longer be an asset to his team? What else was there for him in the Navy? He could train recruits, maybe. If a position opened up.

If he had to go back to Talladega and work at the quarry again, he'd die a slow death. And babysitting spoiled celebrities would be equally soul-crushing. It was different for Neil, he supposed. Neil was in lo— He had a college education. If Clay wanted to teach recruits he would need a four-year degree, at least. As if that would happen.

His stepfather had been right all those years ago.

Clay was dumber than a rock.

And about as useful.

6

"DID YOU LIKE the movie?" James asked Gabby as they exited the theater and strolled down the crowded sidewalk.

"Yes." A nice safe romantic comedy. She doubted either of them could've handled anything violent. A horn honked as a car sped past and she flinched.

It was after eleven at night, but the Manhattan streets still vibrated with yellow cabs and crowds of people hustling to their destinations. Back in her little Texas town, the roads were deserted by ten with the exception of the local sheriff on his nightly patrol.

James reached for her hand, but Gabby lifted it out of his range to pull the edges of her coat tight around herself. "It's gotten chilly since we went in, hasn't it?" She shivered for good measure and then pulled out her phone.

Earlier this evening he'd taken her hand across her tiny kitchen table, but unlike at the park yesterday, she'd casually pulled it away to offer him more enchiladas. James was a nice guy, she supposed, but tonight he'd started to give off a weird vibe.

He'd spent the first several minutes after he arrived at her apartment prowling around, touching things. He'd fingered a few of the books she had crammed on makeshift shelves and stacked on her coffee table. He'd lifted to inspect the few knickknacks she'd brought from home and kept on the two side tables, and opened her blinds to peer out her window. Once, she'd thought he might even try to pull back the curtain to her bedroom.

She was well aware that she had leftover anxiety from the kidnapping. But having James over to her apartment might have been a mistake. It was also possible, however, that she just didn't trust anyone male anymore. Well, except for—no. It wasn't fair to compare James to Clay. She had to stop doing that.

And she had to start living her life in a more meaningful way. But did that mean these vibes she was getting about James were just her psyche's way of making excuses? She hated not being able to trust her instincts.

That wasn't always the case.

When it had come to going away to college, earning her master's and then moving to New York, she hadn't hesitated. Her family had counted on her, and she'd barely given a thought to moving across the country to a new city when it meant being able to help her family.

But when it came to her personal life, she choked.

It *would* be nice to have a boyfriend. Someone special to share every day with. Someone who saw you, and understood you, and cherished you... She turned and stared into James's eyes and tried to imagine what it would be like to kiss him.

But when she thought about James's mouth on hers, her stomach tightened.

Was every guy she tried to date going to have to live up to Clay and that sexy kiss in the jungle?

"I know a good all-night bakery a couple blocks from here. We can get some coffee and doughnuts." James broke into her thoughts.

Good thing he knew the area because she had no clue where they were. The street they'd turned down was less busy. And darker. But she shook off her unease. There were still a few people around. And this was her coworker. A colleague. He, more than anyone else of her acquaintance, knew what it was like to be traumatized. She smiled up at him. "Coffee sounds good."

They walked on, turning another corner. Still holding her coat together with one hand, Gabby opened her Twitter page to comment on the movie and stopped midstep.

Clay Bellamy had started following her? A warm flush traveled up from her chest to her cheeks. He was actually—

"Gabby? Is everything okay?"

She stuck her phone in her pocket. "Yeah, I'm sorry, that was rude." She looked around. "Where are we?"

They'd taken a cab to get to the movie theater, and she could tell they were way on the other side of the Empire State Building from her apartment in the Village. But even after two years she still hadn't completely learned her way around Manhattan. She usually went from her apartment to work and back again. How sad. She really did need to get out and explore the city more.

"—don't you think?"

Gabby bit her lip. What had he asked? She hadn't been listening. "I'm sorry. What were you—?"

"Give me your purse," a gruff voice ordered from the other side of her. Then something sharp jabbed into her and she yelped. The mugger wore a black ski mask and Gabby went into full-blown panic attack, reliving the kidnapping. The world wavered and she couldn't breathe.

"I said give it!" The mugger tried to snatch her purse off her shoulder, wrenching it away from her. In a flash, James stepped between them, grabbed the mugger's wrist and twisted, and the knife clattered to the sidewalk.

Before Gabby even realized it was over, the would-be thief had escaped down the alley.

Gabby's mouth dropped open. James had chased away their attacker? He'd risked his life? Defending her?

"Are you all right?" James was cupping her face.

She tried to slow her breathing and focus her vision. "Yes." She managed to nod and move away from his touch. "I'm okay."

"Are you sure?" He retrieved her purse from the ground and offered it to her.

"I'll be okay." She nodded again, taking the purse.

"I can call 911, but the guy didn't get anything. Should we wait for the police?"

"What could they do now? I think I'd rather go home if you don't mind."

"Sure, no problem." He stepped off the curb and hailed a cab.

On the ride back to her apartment, Gabby fought her instinct to curl into a ball and tried to make conversation. "How were you able to fight off that mugger? That was so brave."

James grinned. "I've been taking self-defense lessons."

Of course. Hadn't she meant to do that? No, Clay had promised to teach her. But that wasn't going to happen now. Had she really thought it would? A pang hit her chest as it always did when she thought of Clay, but she dismissed it. She should look into classes around here.

James paid the cabbie and didn't ask him to wait as he walked her to her apartment building's outer doors. He glanced hopefully up at the windows above before returning his gaze to her. "I had a really good time, Gabby."

Even though they'd been mugged? But she didn't say that. She fished her keys from her purse. Which she still possessed thanks to James. "Thank you for...every—"

James's mouth clamped onto hers, cutting her off. She tried to pull away, but his hand held the back of her head in place. Throwing all her strength into it, she shoved him back.

He stumbled away and she caught a glimpse of fury in his eyes.

That look scared her.

Wiping the back of her hand across her mouth, she turned to unlock the outer door to her building, but her hands shook as she stuck her keys in and he caught her arm. "Hey, I'm really sorry," he said in a pleading voice. "I guess I got the wrong idea. I thought you liked me, you know, that way."

Gabby closed her eyes. She had totally sent him the wrong signals. She couldn't ever be more than friends with James. She slowly turned to face him. "No, *I'm* sorry. I didn't mean to mislead you, James. I thought I could see if it might work, but I don't... I don't feel anything romantic for you. Can we still be friends?"

His expression morphed from penitent to...nothing. The blankness was somehow scarier than the anger. Then it morphed again to a casual smile. "No problem, I mean, sure, of course." He waved a hand. "Don't worry about it. My fault." He seemed so genial that guilt crawled along her insides and landed with a heavy thud in her chest.

With an awkward nod she bolted inside, not waiting to see if he left. She hurried up to her apartment, locked the dead bolt and latched the chain before she felt safe. She dashed to the bathroom and brushed her teeth and gargled with mouthwash, trying to eradicate the taste of James from her mouth.

There were no physical marks from the thief's assault. No visual sign that she'd been mugged. Or almost mugged. But she still thought she might throw up. She reached up to rub her Mary medal, but her hand froze halfway to her neck.

Oh no.

Her medal was gone.

IT WAS CHASING HER!

Sweat dripped into her eyes and she wiped it away as she ran, frantically fighting her way through thick fronds, stumbling, out of breath.

She could hear it coming for her, crashing through the underbrush. It was getting closer, and her feet were stuck, she couldn't move!

Out of nowhere the giant snake jumped out at her, its teeth striking at her, venom dripping from its sharp fangs. She screamed, but no sound came from her mouth. No one would know how she'd died. No one would find her.

Then Clay dropped from a tree and plunged his knife deep into the snake's head and it fell to the ground.

Gabby ran to him and he wrapped his arms around her while she cried and cried. His soft comforting voice, in his slow Southern drawl, told her she was safe now. She could feel his lips on her head, then her cheek, then her mouth...

Gabby woke up with tears on her face and an ache deep in her core. She squeezed her thighs together, rolled to her stomach and cried into her pillow. The terror subsided, but the aching didn't. And she hated that. It was stupid and pointless to want a man she would never see again. She sobbed until she was too tired to be frustrated anymore.

The glow of green numbers on the clock mocked her. Three forty-two. No sense in going back to sleep now. She knew from experience it wouldn't happen.

She pulled herself out of bed, padded to the bathroom and stared at her reflection in the mirror. Was she ever going to get over this? She frowned and splashed cold water on her face. "Get yourself together, Gabriella Diaz," she told herself sternly.

She went to her bedside table and snagged her phone.

@nerdybankanalyst
Another nightmare. Wish I could get past this. Thank goodness for online solitaire. ☺#monstersarenotreal

At work, she headed to the break room for coffee as soon as she exited the elevator. But when her eyes met James's across the coffee pot, his gaze skittered away and he left without pouring himself a cup. No lunch at the park today, she guessed. She felt guilty and irritated at the same time. Why couldn't they just be friends? Now her workplace was going to be uncomfortable.

Eyes stinging, head throbbing, she ignored her sack lunch at noon and laid her cheek down on her folded arms.

Her little hands were pulling up weeds around the shrine. Papa was on his knees beside her, bent over the flower bed. He turned his head and smiled down at her. "Good job, mi hija." She was his helper girl. The summer sun blazed down on them, and she could smell the marigolds and tiger lilies on the breeze. Then a shadow fell across her and she looked up—at James.

She startled awake.

James was standing in her cubicle.

She blinked. "James?"

But he turned and left without saying a word.

Okay, it was official. She'd been right to be creeped out by him. They *weren't* going to be friends.

By five, she was wiped. But instead of going home she studied a map of Manhattan, and then took a train to the Upper West Side, hoping to have time to look for her medal before it got dark. It'd been yanked off when the mugger grabbed her purse strap, she was sure of it.

How many movie theaters could there be north of the Empire State Building? After instructing the cabbie to take her to the north end of Central Park West, she took out her phone and searched for theaters in Manhattan, finally deciding to try the one with a name that sounded familiar.

Once on foot, she followed the route she thought James had taken after leaving the movie and began combing the sidewalk for several blocks, scrutinizing every nook and cranny. She had to find her medal. But anyone could've come along and picked it up since last night. She should've come here this morning, but with all the weekday traffic, she'd been afraid of being late for work.

She walked several more blocks, then turned to retrace her steps and thought she caught someone scurrying into a dim alley. As if the person didn't want to be seen. She shuddered. Had someone been following her? Watching her?

Come on, Gabby. She huffed and shook her head. Paranoid much?

Forcing herself to move past the alley she'd thought the man had ducked into, she continued searching the way she'd come, but no luck. Her heart squeezed. She'd worn the medal since she was six. It was her talisman. Her good luck charm. A symbol of her Abuelita's love.

Now it was gone.

Close to tears, she hailed a cab back to her apartment. As she unlocked the door and let herself in, something felt…off. She slowed her step and made her way down the long hall past her bathroom and into the kitchen.

Around the turn of the twentieth century, her apartment had been three separate hotel rooms with a shared bath down the hall. It was an old building. The wood floors creaked. There was even an old-fashioned transom above the doorway leading into her living room. She turned into her kitchen and, at the small desk in the corner, did a double take. Her laptop was missing. Glancing toward the living room, she lost her breath.

Chaos. As if an earthquake had struck. Her sofa was cut open, books were flung everywhere, knickknacks shattered. Rounding the corner to her curtained-off bedroom, she had to clamp a hand over her mouth to keep from screaming. The bedding had been shredded, her clothes dumped from the drawers.

She ran for the door so fast she tripped on the hall rug and fell against the wall. She was hyperventilating again, but didn't stop until she was down the four flights of stairs and out on the sidewalk. Then she dug in her purse for her cell phone. Her hands shook so hard she had to try three times before punching 911.

By the time the police arrived she'd calmed enough to lead them upstairs and answer the officer's questions. He, of course, assumed it was a routine break-in. But...her television was intact. And who would slash open a sofa? What did the thief think she had hidden in there? Yes, her laptop was missing, but Gabby had a persistent nagging feeling she was being targeted. Which was ridiculous enough that she didn't mention her theory to the policeman.

After a crime scene unit took pictures and dusted for prints, the officer gave her his card, but didn't hold out much hope of finding her laptop. Gabby stood in the middle of her living room, hugging herself, rubbing her arms.

Why was this happening to her? Her job was risk analysis. Statistically, the odds of someone being randomly kidnapped, then mugged and then robbed, all in the space of a month's time weren't impossible. Improbable, yes. But not impossible. And what about that man she'd thought might be following her earlier?

Panic almost overwhelmed her again. But she refused to run. Or succumb to another fit of sobbing. That was how she'd *started* the day. A more productive way to expend her energy would be to start cleaning up. She scanned the living room. Vacuum the glass, duct-tape the sofa—she'd need a new mattress...

She stared at the mess and... She couldn't do it.

She couldn't stay here tonight. But where would

she go? Before last night, she might have called James, but now...?

How sad that, of all the people in this city, she had no one with whom she could ask to stay.

Maybe she should go to a hotel. But they were expensive. Her budget wouldn't stretch to more than one night unless she sent less money home to her parents. And her savings was for true emergencies.

All she knew for sure was that the only time since the kidnapping she'd felt truly safe was in the arms of a stranger. The soldier who rescued her. It wasn't a rational feeling, she knew that. But she felt a connection—a deep, emotional connection to Clay that couldn't be explained. And he had promised to give her self-defense lessons, hadn't he?

"Face it, Gabby." The lessons were just an excuse. Did she seriously think she could just call him up and ask him to teach her how to protect herself? He'd think she was crazy. She didn't even know where he was stationed.

Screw it! She was tired of worrying about why and how and what-ifs. Tired of doing what she should do instead of what she felt like doing. Impulsively, she grabbed her phone and searched for SEAL Team 2... Here was something. US Naval Special Warfare Group 2. Naval Amphibious Base at Little Creek, Virginia Beach! Virginia wasn't that far away. Before she could rethink it, she thumbed the number to call. An automated voice answered and announced that it was after hours and instructed the caller to leave a message at the tone.

Without speaking, she ended the call. What had she expected on a Friday night? She shook her head. It was a wild idea, anyway.

Resigned, she pulled the small broom and dustpan out from under the kitchen sink and hunkered down to sweep up broken glass, but...

The floor blurred as a sense of foreboding crawled below the surface. Like she would go quietly mad if she didn't bolt out the door this instant. Either that or she'd curl up in the corner and never emerge. She drew in a deep breath. "This is just a mild panic attack. Push through it. You'll be fine in a minute."

No, she needed to get out of here!

Grabbing her purse, she dashed down the stairs and outside to hail a cab. She told the cabbie to take her to Penn Station, and once there, she got in line for a ticket.

"Where to?" the old man behind the counter asked.

Gabby drew in a deep breath. She needed to do something to empower herself. To combat the feelings of helplessness and fear. "A round-trip to Virginia Beach, please."

7

"OFFICER BELLAMY?"

At the sound of his name, Clay looked up from his food midchew and frowned. "Here."

The sailor walked to his table and saluted. "Someone's asking for you at the gate, sir."

Asking for him? Here at the base? This couldn't be good. His sister or mom would've texted. Or called, if it was an emergency. He'd talked to Barrow only a few days ago. And anyone else who might want to talk to him was already sitting at this table. His team met at the commissary every Saturday for lunch if they weren't training or deployed.

"Who is it?"

"Female identified herself as…" The sailor looked down at the pink slip of paper. "Ms. Gabriella Diaz, sir."

Gabby. His stomach twitched. Her last Tweet had said something about another nightmare.

"Thank you, Ensign." Clay saluted the messenger, and the kid returned the salute and marched out.

Shorty whistled. "Gabriella! Ooh-la-la."

"You got women meeting you at the base now, Hounddog?" Doughboy smirked and wiggled his brows suggestively.

"What's the matter, you already have a different lady waiting at your place?" Shorty mocked.

Clay got to his feet, nodding and smiling at the razzing. "Yeah, your ex likes meeting at my apartment better than hers."

Chipper snorted as Shorty's grin disappeared.

"Catch y'all later." Keeping his smile in place, Clay grabbed his jacket and lunch tray and sauntered toward the exit.

Gabriella Diaz. Why would Gabby be here asking for him?

As he jumped in his SUV and headed for the front gate, his mind raced trying to come up with a reason she might want to talk to him.

There was that kiss.

Had she become a frog hog? But she hadn't seemed like the groupie type. Besides, it'd been almost a month— three and a half weeks, but who was counting?—since he'd returned her to the American embassy in Paraguay. If she'd developed a thing for SEALs, wouldn't she have shown up before now? No, he knew in his gut Gabby wasn't like that.

Unless she wanted to accuse him of taking advantage.

And maybe he had. He hated thinking he may have caused her any more trauma.

He pulled up to the guardhouse and caught sight of

her standing on the other side of the gate staring out at the vast complex that made up Little Creek. She seemed to be on foot.

She turned and caught sight of him, so he lowered the window and waved as he nodded at the guard to lift the barrier. Driving through, he pulled over to the yellow-striped median just past the guardhouse and got out. "Hey, how you doing?" He slammed the SUV's door behind him and strode over to her.

"Clay?" She was squinting, shielding her eyes from the afternoon sun as he approached.

"Yeah." He lifted his ball cap and ran a hand through his hair, remembering the last time she'd seen him it'd been sheared off to a stubble. He usually grew it longer and let his beard come in just in case he got a covert mission where he needed to blend in.

She, on the other hand, didn't look much different than the last time he'd seen her, other than missing a whole lot of mud. Huddled into a rumpled, threadbare coat, she wore sensible flats, no makeup and no jewelry. Her long dark hair was tied back in a disheveled ponytail. As he watched, she smoothed a stray strand behind her ear and pulled the coat tighter around her.

She sure wasn't dressed to entice. In fact, she seemed as if she'd lost some of her spit and fire. There were dark circles under her eyes and a gauntness to her cheeks. Nightmares would do that to a person.

But there was still a sensual quality about her. It wasn't just the curvy bod he knew was beneath the bulky coat. Or the full lips and big chocolate-brown eyes. It was...nothing he could explain.

"How did you get here?"

"I took a train and then a bus." She gestured vaguely at the bus depot a couple of blocks from the gate.

"Ah." He nodded, scanning the area out of habit. Finally, he looked into her eyes. And the awkwardness fell away. She was just Gabby. And something was wrong. "What's happened?" he asked without thinking.

"I, uh…" Her face crumpled and she covered her mouth with her palm.

"Hey, it's okay." He stepped closer and put an arm around her shoulders, and she buried her face against his chest and started sobbing.

"What the—?" Clay glanced back at the guard, then down at the woman crying uncontrollably. His only interaction with females usually involved flirting and spending a few hours in mutually satisfying sex.

Aw, hell. He wrapped his other arm around her and rubbed her back, making shushing noises. "Hey, now. It's okay." He bent a knuckle under her chin and lifted her face to look at him. "Kidnapped, shot at, almost bit by a snake and not one tear. But go a month without me and it's waterworks city, huh?"

She snorted a watery laugh and he felt like the king of the world.

"Let's go somewhere we can talk, okay?"

At her nod, he guided her to his SUV. One thing different about her, she smelled good. A sweet, flowery fragrance that reminded him of something from his past. He couldn't quite put a name to it, but it lingered in the back of his mind as he closed the door and went around to the driver's side.

The burger joint on the corner was too public, but Barney's would be fairly deserted at this time of day. While she dug some tissues out of her purse and cleaned up, he drove down the street to the mostly empty pool hall on the wharf, escorted her to a booth in the back and ordered two coffees from the waitress.

After Gabby shrugged out of her coat and blotted her cheeks with a napkin, she sniffled and let out a long sigh. "I'm sorry. You must think I'm a lunatic to show up here like this." She rolled her eyes and shook her head.

"Uh, well." What could he say? Except the woman he'd gotten to know in that jungle wasn't the kind to wimp out over nothing. Something was going on. "It can be tough coming through something like you did. Takes time."

"True, but—I shouldn't have bothered you."

She looked so vulnerable. So worried. He gestured to the mug in front of her. "Drink your coffee."

After biting her bottom lip—a luscious bottom lip—she started tearing open sugar packets and dumping them into her coffee. "Do they have, like, food here, because I'm starving?" She finally met his gaze. "Can I buy you lunch?"

There was that fighting spirit. The strength that had gotten her to rally after every setback in the jungle. "I already ate. But they have nachos and stuff." He waved the waitress over to take Gabby's order. Gabby smiled shyly at the waitress and avoided eye contact with him.

Deciding she'd talk when she was ready, he settled in, draped his arm across the back of the booth and watched her sip her coffee. His attention fixed on her lips. In a rush of unwanted emotion he recalled that night in the jungle. The intimacy of total darkness. How she'd trusted him so completely. How she'd kissed him as if she couldn't live one more minute without her mouth on his.

How badly he'd wanted to forget all his training and give in.

With a wince she set her mug down. "It sounds silly now, but, I came down here to ask you to teach me those self-defense moves like you promised."

Clay blinked. She'd traveled twelve hours from New York to Virginia for self-defense lessons? He cleared his throat. "They don't have any martial arts studios back in Manhattan?"

She studied the paper napkin as she shredded it. "See? I told you I was a lunatic to come here." Splotches of pink appeared on her cheeks to match the redness on the tip of her cute little nose.

"No, it's just that—"

The waitress set the plate of nachos on the table. "Need anything else, hon?"

Gabby smiled up at the woman. "No, this looks great, thanks." Her smile faded after the waitress shuffled off.

"What's really going on? There's something you're not telling me."

She looked up from her balled-up napkin, her eyes troubled, hesitant.

"Don't worry if it sounds crazy. Let me be the judge of that." He stole a nacho.

Her lungs seemed to deflate. "It's probably a coincidence. Or bad luck. I mean, I wasn't even going to get into that cab until Mr. V asked me to join him. And people get mugged in New York every day. Probably. And apartments get robbed all the time. Right?" Her eyes pleaded for reassurance.

Clay pieced together what she was saying. She'd been mugged? Robbed? She hadn't mentioned that in any of her Tweets. "You think you're the target of some...plot? That you, specifically, were supposed to be kidnapped? Do you have some fortune or powerful relative? And wouldn't the kidnappers have contacted them instead of the bank for the ransom?"

Gabby shook her head. "No, you're right. It doesn't make any sense, does it? It must be horribly bad luck."

Clay narrowed his eyes, thinking. Gabby didn't strike him as the type to imagine or invent crises. She wasn't even close to being mentally unstable. But he had some experience with post-traumatic stress. "Tell me about these other two incidents. You were mugged and your apartment was broken into?"

"Yes, but, like you said, why me? I'm nobody."

"You're not nobody." The words slipped out before he thought them through. There was an awkward silence while she stared at him.

"The worst thing was losing my medal." Her fingers touched her bare collarbone.

"It was stolen?"

"I don't think so. It probably just broke off when he grabbed my purse."

Grabbed her purse. He pictured Gabby, alone, vulnerable, attacked. Clay wished he'd been there to protect her, pictured himself beating the daylights out of the creep who dared threaten her.

Whoa. He unclenched his fists and leaned forward, elbows on the table between them. "Are you okay? Were you hurt?"

"No, only frightened. He—he had a knife. But he didn't hurt me."

Clay's heart thumped at the word *knife*.

She gave a halfhearted smile and reached for a nacho, but didn't eat it. "I panicked yesterday. Walked into my apartment after work and found it ransacked. Maybe I wouldn't have felt quite so violated if the kidnapping hadn't happened. I should've called the therapist I've been talking to. And I do need to take some self-defense lessons when I get back. They sure helped James."

A thought struck and he swallowed a bad taste. "Is that your...boyfriend? Fiancé?"

"No!" She stared at the nacho between her fingers. "He's a colleague. You met him. The guy who was kidnapped with me."

That sniveling coward? But Clay sipped his coffee and kept his opinion to himself. Sounded like she had every right to be a little panicked. Two attacks in less than a month. And both right on the heels of the kidnapping. That was some run of bad luck. He rubbed the whiskers on his chin. Something felt hinky about that. Maybe he'd get Neil to look into it for him.

Wrong.

He should stay out of it. Send her back to New York

now. There were a couple of places there he could recommend that taught self-defense. Reputable dojos where she could learn to fend off most attacks. He didn't need to get involved with this. Why had she come to him, anyway? She barely knew him.

But the creep had pulled a knife on her. Someone had broken into her apartment. What must it have taken for her to get on a train alone last night and travel over three hundred miles to ask him for help? He wasn't going to let that be for nothing. "Since you're already here, I could show you a couple of moves to protect yourself."

"You could?" The appreciation in her eyes landed a blow to his gut. He didn't want it. Didn't sit well.

It was Saturday afternoon. A check of his watch told him it was a little before fourteen-hundred hours. His team would've gone their separate ways by now. He shrugged. "You caught me at a good time. I'm on standby. Waiting around to be deployed." He could play pool and drink beer with the guys anytime.

"You don't need to be on the base to do that?"

"As long as I stay close, we're good."

And there was that smile. Her expression lit her whole face. The look that said he was amazing.

And damned if he didn't want to believe it.

"Let's get out of here." Tossing some bills on the table, Clay held Gabby's coat while she stuck her arms in the sleeves, and then escorted her out to his SUV. The biting wind off the Atlantic blew a few more strands loose from her ponytail and he had a moment's wish to see it loose and falling over her shoulders.

She climbed in, shivering, so Clay turned the seat warmers on and the heater up full blast. With a sigh, she leaned her head back on the headrest and closed her eyes. Her whole body relaxed.

"You been sleeping okay?"

She lifted her head and opened her eyes. "The train ride was bumpy."

He raised a skeptical brow. But he didn't want to admit he read her Tweets. He gave his attention back to the road and tugged the bill of his ball cap lower over his eyes. He should probably take her to her hotel first to change and drop off her— "Where's your bag? Where are you staying?"

"Oh. I didn't—didn't pack anything. I wasn't thinking very clearly when I left. All my clothes were scattered on the floor, and there was broken glass, and—and dumped food. I just…couldn't."

She needed better security in that apartment. He made a mental note to talk to Neil about it. Apparently, she hadn't made a hotel reservation either. He swallowed. Maybe she was planning on returning to New York tonight.

He made a quick right turn into a strip mall and parked in front of a sporting goods store. He pulled out the key and set the brake. "As with any plan of attack, the first thing you need is the right gear."

Her brows crinkled, but, like the trooper she was, she followed him inside, no questions asked.

With only a general order to choose some comfortable workout clothes, he left her in Ladies' clothing and headed for the camping and fishing section. When he caught up with her at the checkout, she'd purchased a pair of soft gray sweatpants and a matching cotton T-shirt. "Here." He handed her the pepper spray on a quick-release key ring he'd bought her.

"Oh, thank you." Her face lit up as she smiled at him. "I feel safer already." Seeing her with her dark brown eyes twinkling and her honey-brown skin flushed from the store's heat, his body reacted in ways that would make close contact with her probably not a good idea.

Why was he doing this to himself?

But he couldn't back out now.

A short ride later he pulled into his apartment complex. At her questioning look, he tried to reassure her. "My apartment was the only place I could think of for these lessons besides the gym at the base, and we don't have time to get you clearance."

"Oh, right." She nodded.

As they walked up to his second-floor efficiency, he tried to remember exactly how messy he'd left it this morning. But the sofa and recliner were free of clothes and the coffee table only had last night's pizza box and beer can. Not too bad.

With a muttered apology, he rushed to dump it all in the trash, but she waved it off as no big deal, complimented his sparse, builder-grade decor as a "nice place" and asked directions to the bathroom.

Looking around, he took off his jacket and boots, then shoved the coffee table over to a wall and dragged in his punching bag from the bedroom.

"Ready?" he asked as she came into the living room.

Though she spread her feet and nodded confidently,

he noticed she ran her palms nervously down the front of her sweatpants. *Back atcha, Gabriella Diaz.*

Why should he be nervous? All he had to do was show her a few defensive moves and then take her back to the train station. Or a hotel. Either one. Made no difference to him. He rubbed the back of his neck. "Okay, so show me how the mugger came at you with the knife."

Gabby's breathing hitched and her face looked stricken.

Oh, wow. He moved close, took her shoulders. "You can do this. Look at me." He softly stroked her cheek with the back of his fingers.

She looked up into his eyes and he realized he was rubbing her arm, as well.

He dropped his hands and stepped back. "*You're* the one in control now, right?"

With a slight nod she seemed to rally. "Right." She took a deep breath. "He—he just appeared from an alleyway and held it against my side." She pointed to her right side, about the middle of her rib cage.

He grimaced. "Close quarters, then. Without a lot of training, the best thing you can do is run. Put as much distance between you and the weapon as possible. Now, if he lunges at you, you *could* try to shove his arm away." He took her wrist and lifted her arm to mimic her jabbing a knife at him, and, in one swift move, demonstrated slamming it away with the heel of his hand, which brought her chest to chest with him.

Her soft, rounded chest.

And she was looking at him with her mouth open, her lips a circle of luscious pink flesh.

His mind blanked. All he could think about was how

good she smelled. How near she was. How her breasts felt pressed against him.

He let her wrist go and backed away. "Uh, the best thing is to have your pepper spray out and ready. Spray him and then run."

She nodded. "Run, check."

What could he show her, then? Hand-to-hand, blocking... "Okay, how to get out of a hold." He extended his arm toward her. "Grab my wrist."

She circled his wrist with her hand, but he immediately twisted out of her grasp.

"The weakest part of your attacker's grip is where his thumb meets his fingers, so all you have to do is twist and jerk your arm free in whatever direction his thumb is facing. Now you try it." He grabbed her wrist. It was so small and delicate.

She met his gaze, waiting for his signal.

"Jerk it away." He shook her wrist and gripped it tighter, and she wrenched her arm away from his thumb, and like that she was free.

She smiled. "It worked!"

That smile would be the death of him. He nodded. "Try it again." He grabbed her other wrist from a different direction and when she tried to wrench out of his hold, she couldn't. He shook his head. "My thumb was in a different place this time."

"Oh." She frowned. "Right." She yanked the other way and escaped.

"Good. Now, the most vulnerable parts on the body are knees, nose, eyes and groin. He pointed to each area as he spoke, motioning last to the zippered area of his jeans. Then he led her over to the punching bag and demonstrated how he wanted her to turn sideways and kick the punching bag. "Pretend you're aiming for a knee." He grabbed her hands. "Get your arms up like a fighter, make a fist, that's it. Now kick."

Gabby toed off her shoes, kicked and glanced back at him. "Like that?"

"That was good, but really throw your weight into it by twisting from the waist."

After she'd kicked the bag again and again, grunting louder with each kick, he had her punch the bag with her fists, then jab it up high with the heel of her hand as if she was going for a nose.

"Not bad, but—" He moved behind her. "Transfer your weight from your back foot to your front foot." He put one hand at her waist, gripped the elbow and moved it forward to simulate the jab, but he felt her stiffen at his touch.

He backed off, gritting his teeth. Had he scared her? "Try it again."

After about a dozen more hits, jabs and punches, she turned to face him, breathing heavily. "Yes!" She planted her hands on her hips, and bounced from foot to foot, smiling. "That felt so good. I'm so glad I'm doing this!"

Clay's attention was riveted on her chest as it rose and fell, and on her swaying hips. She had no idea how provocative her movements were and that turned him on even more. He forced himself to look away.

"Can you show me what to do if someone grabs me from behind?"

Like you just did. Clay heard her unspoken words. She hadn't wanted him coming up on her from behind like that. Well, he was just as uncomfortable touching her as she was being touched. Although he was pretty sure it was for completely different reasons. Just thinking about fitting snugly against her backside…

"Clay?"

He needed a cold shower. "Okay, so…" Slowly, he moved into position behind her. *Think about something else, Bellamy.* The hypothermia of Hell Week. Or the month he froze his butt off training in winter warfare in Sweden. Gritting his teeth, he reached his arms around her and pinned her arms to her body. Her scent did things to his brain function. "What you want to do is move your hips to one side."

She cocked her hip to her right. "Like this?" She glanced up and behind her and their lips almost touched.

He froze a moment, his gaze on her mouth. If he lowered his head a mere half an inch… Her lips parted and he closed his eyes, breathing in. "What is that perfume?" he mumbled, eyes still closed.

"Gardenia. My grandmother wore it."

Her grandmother. Clay snapped out of his lust. He remembered she'd talked about her family that day in the jungle. About her parents and siblings. She was close with her family. And a virgin.

White picket fence, remember, Bellamy?

Putting some space between them, he took her left hand and curled his fingers over hers, making a fist. "After you move your hip to the side, punch back to his groin." He swung her arm back forcefully, stopping just short of his jeans. "You can slap, punch, even grab his you-know-what and twist."

"Okay." She nodded and stared at their hands, his larger one wrapped around hers. "You smell nice, too."

Clay almost groaned out loud.

When he didn't respond, she pulled her hand away and started to step forward, but he tugged her back against him. "Let's say he's got you really low and tight." He bent his knees and dropped his arms lower around her hips, his chin touching her shoulder. He heard her gasp, and thought he'd scared her, but she leaned back into him with a tiny moan. Wait, what? Maybe her reaction wasn't fear.

"Clay?" Her voice sounded breathy.

"What?" If he turned his face he could nuzzle her neck right behind her soft little earlobe.

She turned to look him in the eye. "What do I do now?"

He swallowed. His lips parted. *You kiss me like you did that night in the jungle and then we make love right here on the floor.*

He cleared his throat. "If your lower arms are pinned, you stomp as hard as you can on the top of his foot, even kick back to hit his shin. But the top of the foot has a lot of little bones and it hurts like hell."

Ready to put more distance between them, he let her go and stepped away. "Remember, go for the knee or the top of the foot, and then run. Kicking those areas will keep the guy from being able to chase you. Your goal here is not to actually bring him down, but to do just enough to get away. You strike, and then you run, okay?"

"Got it. Strike and run."

"That's enough for a first lesson. Want something to drink?" He went to the fridge for a couple of bottles of water. Maybe he'd pour one over his head. Or splash it on something lower. "When you get back, find a gym or a dojo and practice regularly." He handed her a water.

Nodding, she took it. "I will."

They both sipped their water in silence.

"Clay?"

"Yeah." He finally refocused on her face.

She stared at him, rolled her lips in and then bit the bottom one.

Wow, those lips.

She moved closer. Another step toward him.

Agitation seized his gut.

With a wince, she squeezed her eyes shut. "What if an attacker has me pinned on the ground?"

Had the kidnappers tried to assault her? He wanted to hit something. Hard.

She needed to be able to defend herself. And he wanted to make sure she could never be hurt again. But how could he be sure she would feel safe when part of him—in fact, most of him—wanted her himself? There was no way he could show her these moves without her knowing exactly what she did to him.

In his mind, he heard the quarry's strident alarm-bell buzzing—the signal for danger. His lips flattened. "Lie on your back, arms above your head."

8

WHAT WAS SHE DOING?

Gabby contemplated telling Clay she'd changed her mind.

Panic, post-traumatic stress and sleepless nights had led to some terrible decisions on her part lately. Like running away from her life just because she'd had a few scary incidents. Like using those incidents as a flimsy excuse to track down a guy she barely knew. And now here she was trying to seduce said guy.

Clay was scowling, looking, even out of uniform, like the hardened soldier she'd first met in the jungle. Confident. Unwavering. A man to be reckoned with.

She might have thought she was coming to see him in order to feel safe. But if that was the truth, it wasn't the whole truth. Now that she was here—in the presence of Clay's hard-muscled, tight T-shirt and jeans-clad body—she knew exactly what she wanted.

She wanted him. She wanted to finish what they'd started back in that jungle in Paraguay. And she thought—hoped—that he wanted the same thing. She definitely felt something—some…spark between them. And that spark encouraged her.

Terrible decision or not, Gabby dropped to the floor, flipped onto her back and laid her hands on either side of her head. Her stomach was turning somersaults, or maybe it was a place slightly lower.

With a quick flick of her wrist, she yanked the band from her ponytail and shook out her hair. His gaze followed her motion. He was watching her with a banked hunger in his eyes. But banked embers could be coaxed into flames.

He dropped to all fours and positioned himself over her, straddling her waist. She felt a moment's shock, but it wasn't a bad feeling. She wasn't afraid. Never afraid with Clay.

"If a guy has your hands pinned." He leaned forward and lightly clasped her wrists, but his eyes lowered to her chest. Her nipples tightened. She wanted to beg for his touch. When she took a breath, her stomach rose against his hard…zipper.

A muscle ticked in his jaw as he lifted his gaze to her face. "You can still throw off an attacker. First, raise your knees and plant your feet wide."

Obeying his instructions, her thighs snugged up against his butt.

"Now, move your left wrist away from your head." He demonstrated extending her arm all the way out and how, because he was gripping her wrist it caused him to pitch forward and to her left. "See? That throws me off balance because my hand goes out from under me."

"Oh, cool. Let me try that again." With his fingers still encircling her wrist, she replicated the move and he fell forward a second time. Now they were chest to chest. With only the thin cotton of their shirts between them. His hardness pressed to her softness. Everywhere.

She took a deep breath and licked her lips. His eyes were a whiskey brown. His lips... She wanted to lift her head and catch them with her own. Just to see if they were as supple as they looked.

She understood that she had to go back to her apartment and deal with her life. She wasn't expecting till death did they part. But before she returned to reality, at the very least she wanted a kiss. One last kiss from him when she wasn't covered in mud, filth and bug bites. Just to see if kissing him was as all-consuming as she remembered. She raised her head...

He straightened abruptly, moving her wrist back beside her head. "That was good." At least his voice was raspy. "Now, when you throw me off balance, raise your right hip to shove me off." He bent over her and encircled her wrists in a tighter clasp, his face grim.

She waited a heartbeat, and then tried it.

It worked and he pitched off to her side. Emboldened, she rolled on top of him, grabbed his wrists and shackled them to the floor.

His eyes flared, and then narrowed. But he didn't fight her.

Before he could, she took his mouth in hers. She refused to lose this moment to timidity.

After a stunned second he returned her kiss, his lips moving over hers, nipping, sucking, tasting.

She lifted her head and stared into his eyes. She was no longer holding his wrists. Somehow their fingers had entwined. As weird as it seemed, Gabby thought the rest of her life might be determined by what Clay did next… Then with a gruff moan he rolled again, gathered her up in his arms and kissed her, hard and ravenously.

Needing to touch him, she clasped his jaw, tangled her fingers in his hair. She was drowning in the feel of his mouth on hers, taking and giving, plundering, teasing inside with his tongue. She started untucking his T-shirt from his belt and inching it up his back, running her palms over the hot, bare skin on either side of his spine. She wanted to feel him everywhere, feel his skin against hers, and their clothes were *so* in the way.

His lips moved down her jawline to the hollow of her throat, kissing, licking. His rough beard scratched her. When his mouth reached the edge of her V-neck she cried out her encouragement and squirmed beneath him. Her shirt had to go. And so did his.

Impatient, she yanked his T-shirt up over his head and he lifted away long enough to finish pulling it off and tossing it. While he did that she grabbed the hem of her shirt and had barely gotten it off before his mouth landed at the edge of her bra, pressing kisses between her breasts.

Before she could do it herself, he'd reached behind her to unsnap her bra, and they tussled to see which one could drag the straps down her arms faster before he suckled one hardened nipple.

She gave a tiny yelp. The sensation of his teeth scraping one tip and then the other was a pleasure more intense than anything she'd ever felt. As his hands and mouth caressed her breasts, all she could do was feel, and all she could feel was a desire so powerful it overwhelmed her.

With a wet pop, he let go of her nipple and spread openmouthed kisses down her stomach. One hand still clutched her breast, but the other was sliding under the elastic of her sweatpants, tugging them down along with her panties as he stroked her hip, then her butt.

She lifted her hips to him, offering him whatever he wanted. "Clay. I've wanted this—wanted you, ever since that night."

He stilled, his mouth open on the sensitive skin inches below her naval. His warm breath tickled in harsh puffs as he panted above her. Slowly, he withdrew his hand, righted the waistband of her sweatpants and pushed up to his knees.

Wait. No. Don't get up. Gabby almost said the words out loud. But she could tell by the set of his jaw it would've been a waste of breath. He avoided her eyes as he got to his feet, his fists clenched at his sides. "This was a mistake."

Bam. Sucker punch to the gut. She lost her breath, didn't know where to look. Her nipples were still wet from his tongue. As he turned away, she reached for her shirt so she could cover her breasts. Her vision tunneled and she barely heard him mutter something about being back in a bit as she ran for the bathroom.

WHAT HAD HE DONE?

Clay paid for the Chinese food, grabbed the brown paper sack and slid behind the wheel of his SUV.

Geez, he'd almost taken Gabby's virginity. Good thing he'd snapped out of it. One more minute and he'd have had their pants off and taken her right there on his living room floor. Not a great place for a lady's first time.

And he definitely wasn't the right partner for a lady's first time either. She was no teenager. If she'd waited this long, sex must be important, must mean something more to her than scratching an itch. She deserved more than a quick romp with a virtual stranger. And that's all tonight would've been.

She was just scared right now. Not thinking straight from all the crap she'd been through. And he sure wasn't about to take advantage of her post-trauma vulnerability.

But now he had to face her after the way he'd left things... Not his finest moment.

The sun was sitting on the horizon, leaving the sky a murky twilight when he returned to the apartment, got to his door and turned the key in the lock. No lights on inside. "Gabby?"

No answer.

He flipped on the overhead light, but didn't see her. Had she—? Alarm subsided as he stepped in and caught sight of her curled up on his couch. She'd fallen asleep.

She must've crashed hard because neither the light nor his boot steps had woken her.

Guilty and relieved at the same time, he stuck the food in the fridge and grabbed a beer, then stood drinking it while he studied his troublesome guest.

His chest ached watching her sleep. He didn't think it

possible but she looked even more innocent with one hand tucked under her chin, her long dark hair mussed over her face, her lush mouth open. He was going to have a hard time getting that image out of his head. Not to mention how she'd looked earlier, her large pinkish-brown nipples, shiny from his mouth, or how her dark skin had smelled of gardenias, how she'd writhed beneath him.

Face it. The time he'd spent away, willing his body to cool off, had been a complete waste. He clenched his fists to keep from dragging her into his arms.

She mumbled something and fidgeted, and he remembered how she'd talked in her sleep that night in the jungle. Stalking to his bedroom, he yanked the comforter off his bed and dragged it back to spread over her. She snuggled in deeper.

She was so sweet, lying there quietly. If he didn't do something to make sure she was safe, he might not be able to let her go home in the morning. And he *had* to get her out of here.

Turning away, he pulled out his cell and dialed Neil. The least he could do was have a security system set up in her apartment. When his buddy's voice mail answered, Clay left a message. "Hey, Barrow. I need a favor. Call me when you get this." He stared at her again. First thing tomorrow he'd deliver her to the train station.

Gulping his beer, he headed for his bedroom.

He needed another beer. But first he'd take a long, cold shower.

THE FIRST THING Gabby realized as she slowly awoke was that her left hand was asleep. The second was that she had actually slept long enough for something to go numb.

The third thing she realized, as she opened her eyes and her brain snapped fully alert, was that she wasn't in her bed.

"I told you. I can't get away right now." Clay's voice.

Gabby focused beyond the sofa pillow her face was smashed against and saw Clay standing in front of the living room window, speaking on his cell phone. Even with his profile silhouetted against the window's blinds she could tell he was scowling.

"Don't lay that guilt on me. It won't work. I'm not coming, all right?"

Who was he talking to? Whoever it was inspired a deep-seated resentment in him. Or perhaps it was the subject matter. Either way, Gabby could hear the bitter anger in his tone.

"Look, there's nothing I can do. I'll talk to you later, okay?" He clicked off and swung to face Gabby.

Their gazes met and she blinked. The sheer physicality of him made her stomach dip. He wore running clothes and his T-shirt was damp in the center of his chest. He'd been jogging, presumably. A morning person, then. Whereas she could easily sleep for several more hours. How long had she been asleep, anyway? And wasn't this Sund—

The events of last night leaped to mind. Humiliation swamped her and she jackknifed up and the blanket slid to the floor.

Clay bent to grab it at the same time she did, then let go as their hands touched.

Where was an invisibility cape when you needed one?

The last time she'd felt this mortified had also been the result of a rash decision. She'd once tried happy hour with some of the women from her office. After a few drinks she'd decided twenty-five was way too old to still be a virgin and had left with a cute guy. Luckily, he'd been unexpectedly understanding when she broke off a hot and heavy kiss at his door and told him she'd changed her mind.

She'd wished for a cloaking device at that moment.

But this time was worse.

This time it hadn't been her idea to stop.

"Bagel or Danish?" Clay offered her a white pastry bag she hadn't noticed him holding before. The thought of food and the delicious aroma of coffee made her stomach gurgle. Apparently, even acute embarrassment wasn't enough to kill her appetite.

Gabby swiped the hair out of her face. The train! She jumped to her feet. She had to get home. "What time is it?"

He checked his watch. "Oh-seven-hundred."

"I—I need to get to the train station. Is there a bus stop close by?"

"Gabby." He said her name with an air of disappointment. "I'll take you to the train station. But you have time to eat. Grab a shower even."

She eyed the pastry bag. She *was* starving. But given the way they'd left things last night, how could he act so casual? She couldn't even stand to think about how she'd thrown herself at him. And how he'd rejected her.

"Look, about last night." His face was expression-less. "I didn't handle that well. It's just that—"

"No need to explain," she interjected. "I get it." She started folding the thick duvet, straightening the pil-lows on his sofa, collecting her stuff. Anything to avoid eye contact.

"No, I'm pretty sure you don't, Gabby. I'm a SEAL. And SEALs—"

"Please." She finally looked at him, pleading. "I re-ally don't want to talk about it."

His mouth tightened and the corners dropped into a frown. "Okay."

"Thank you." She set the folded blanket on the couch and headed down the hall. "I'll be ready to go in thirty minutes, if that's okay."

The next hour was excruciatingly civil. The uncom-fortable silence in his SUV made the short ride to the train station seem like hours. And once they arrived there he insisted on walking with her to the platform.

While she'd wolfed down a Danish, he'd showered and dressed in crisp brown-and-tan camouflage pants with a dark brown T-shirt, though he hadn't shaved. He studied the train arrival and departure schedule, checked his watch and then finally turned to look at her. "Be sure to practice those moves once you get back."

"I will." She fussed with her purse, digging out her return ticket.

A moment of silence passed.

You have to face him sometime, coward. She smoothed out her ticket and then looked him in the eye. "Thank you for taking the time to teach me."

He nodded, took her phone and thumbed in something. "It's my cell number," he said, handing it back. "Feel free to call if you need anything." Then he winced and half turned away.

Yeah, that would happen. She stuck out her right hand. "Thanks again." *Have a nice life.*

When he finally met her eyes she felt the predictable punch of desire. "Take care." He gave her hand a hard, quick shake, then strode off.

Well.

Now she knew exactly how James had felt. Friend zoned.

But on the train ride home, her phone beeped, signaling the battery was dying. That reminded her of Clay this morning when he'd been talking on his phone. He'd been telling someone he couldn't get away. That he didn't want to be guilted into something.

Whoever he'd been talking to bothered him more than he let on.

9

@nerdybankanalyst
Self-defense lessons awesome. Thank you, you-know-who #bankingpunoftheday Two banks with different rates have a conflict of interest.

"MEETING'S ADJOURNED. Thank you, everyone." The new vice president stood and all the project managers around the table got to their feet, collecting papers and folders.

Finally. Gabby was on her third mug of coffee this morning already. The train from Virginia Beach hadn't arrived at Penn Station until well after midnight and getting to sleep in the vandalized apartment had been a challenge. Although, the self-defense lessons must've helped some. She'd slept without nightmares.

As people began to file out, Gabby uncrossed her legs and slipped her notepad under her stack of reports. Probably not a good idea to let the new VP see she'd been doodling on her legal pad for the past ten minutes.

She'd never been sure why she even needed to attend these weekly meetings, but the enormous conference room had a spectacular view of the Freedom Tower. Plus...doughnuts. Who was she to question her superiors?

"Ms. Diaz, can I talk to you for a sec?"

Gabby froze, and then faced her supervisor, Pamela Cloud. "Yes, ma'am?"

"One of our senior analysts has a family emergency. How would you feel about attending the International Banking Conference next week?"

Um...elated? Excited? Over the moon? Was she kidding? They were talking Switzerland here. Every year bankers from around the world convened in Lucerne. Gabby would give her eyeteeth to go. "Me?"

"Yes, you." Her boss smiled. "You've proven yourself competent, hardworking and, most of all—" she leaned in conspiratorially and lowered her voice "—I need someone who will actually attend the workshops instead of spending the whole trip sampling the beer and eating schnitzel."

"Gabby's going?" James blurted out, appearing beside her.

Gabby jumped, but Pamela glared at him. His pale complexion reddened and he stammered something about being glad she would have the opportunity. But he didn't look glad. Was he simply surprised that a junior analyst was going? Or was he specifically unhappy that *she* would be there? Maybe he'd looked forward to going to the conference without her.

She'd avoided seeing him in the break room this morning as usual, and he'd given her the cold shoulder when she'd been forced to sit beside him at this meeting. So far this month, she was two-for-two in the alienating-men category. *Go me*.

Despite that, she couldn't tamp down a ripple of excitement about the trip to Switzerland. It meant she might get a little closer to receiving the promotion—and raise—she'd been hoping for. The extra money would really help Jorge's college fund.

After instructing Gabby to watch for flight and other details about the trip in her inbox, Pamela left, but James lingered. "Congratulations. They've never sent a ~~analyst~~ to Lucerne before." He smiled, but there ~~feel~~ to his well-wishes.

Still, ~~to~~ think the best of him. "Thanks," she said, returning his smile. Maybe asking his advice would boost his ego. Since they had to work together, she did want to be on friendly terms with him. "You went last year. What clothes should I pack for April in Switzerland?"

He looked shocked. "How would I know what clothes you have?" He smoothed his hair down at the front and back, and hurried out.

Gabby blinked. Maybe the incident in Paraguay had left him a burrito short of a fiesta platter.

As soon as she got home she turned on her favorite telenovela while she started cleaning up the mess in her apartment. She'd been too exhausted earlier to do anything but fall into bed. As she grabbed up clothes and books, she made a mental list of what she would take to Switzerland. That helped the heartache of finding some of her favorite novels ripped apart. "You just need to put the break-in and the humiliation of the last two days behind you, Gabby Diaz."

She'd cleared most of the chaos from the living room, and made a mental note to buy a sofa cover, when her buzzer rang. At the same time her phone beeped announcing that she had a text.

Grabbing her phone, she answered the door buzzer first. "Who is it?"

"Neil Barrow, Barrow Security. Clay sent me, Ms. Diaz."

At Clay's name, Gabby's stomach leaped. "Cl you for what?" She couldn't even begin

"He should've sent a text expla

The text. She checked her

Barrow is ex-SEAL. Owed me a favor.
Will beef up security for you.
Ask him for code word.
He should tell you: straight arrow

"Ms. Diaz?" the man on the intercom prompted.

Gabby realized her mouth was hanging open and pressed her intercom button. "What's the code word?"

"Straight arrow."

Was this for real? Should she let this stranger inside her apartment? What had he said his company name was? Maybe she could do a quick search for it on her phone. She found a website for Barrow Security. Wow. He *was* an ex-SEAL. And a bodyguard to lingerie model Piper.

She pressed the button to let him in and a minute

later she heard the old elevator squeaking its way up. Gabby rushed to the bathroom to brush her hair and touch up her makeup, and then made a face at herself in the mirror. Did she think this guy was going to report back to Clay on her appearance?

Shaking her head, she darted back to the door just as someone knocked. She checked the peephole and spied a tall guy with an average build and light brown hair. He didn't wear any kind of uniform, just jeans and a button-down dress shirt. Nothing menacing about him, except he carried a bulky, black leather duffel…

When she didn't answer right away, he set down the duffel, pulled out his wallet and held up an identification card with his credentials. Certified by the Department of Homeland Security? She unlocked the dead bolt, unhooked the chain and swung the door open, greeting him with a handshake.

"Neil Barrow. Nice to meet you, ma'am." He had that same military bearing that distinguished Clay from other men.

"Just Gabby." She bit her lip.

"I've known Clay since BUD/S—er, basic training," he said, shouldering the bag. "He was worried about your apartment's security and asked me to install a few alarms and cameras."

"He is? He did?"

"Yes, ma'am, uh, Gabby." He smiled ruefully. "And I owe him a favor, so there's no charge. Take maybe a couple of hours."

Clay had called in a favor from a former Navy SEAL who now guarded a famous model? Because he was worried about her? Maybe she shouldn't read into that, but she couldn't help a little flicker of hope that Clay really had felt something for her.

Or maybe he just felt guilty.

Which he shouldn't. He hadn't done anything wrong. The whole mess had been her fault.

"So...?" the guy urged.

Oh, gosh, the man was still waiting in the hallway. She smiled and ushered him in, leading him down the hall. "I guess you can see what would be best. I don't want to be any trouble, though." And she'd have to Tweet another thank-you to one of her followers later.

When she turned back to the ex-SEAL, he'd detoured into her small kitchen—stepping over dumped drawers and cabinets—before coming to stand in the middle of her living room.

He wore a grim expression as he looked around. "Bellamy said someone broke in, but he didn't mention the slashed sofa and ruined personal items."

That was because *she* hadn't mentioned them to Clay. "Happens all the time, right?"

The security guy raised a dubious brow and then gestured to the alcove that was her bedroom. "May I?"

At her nod, he strode past the curtain, and she heard him swear under his breath. The slashed underwear *was* kind of...creepy. One of the reasons she'd panicked the other night.

He reappeared and stared at her, hard. "This wasn't some random break-in, Gabby."

The hairs on her arms stood up. "What do you mean?"

The ex-SEAL's eyes narrowed. "Someone hates you."

CLAY BIT THE inside of his cheek to keep from doubling over in pain. That last punch to the solar plexus hurt like a son of a gun.

He'd spent the day on base punishing his body. Training at the gym with his buddies, then going a few rounds in the ring with a young hotshot who'd probably be taking Clay's place in his SEAL team in the next couple of years. That was a sobering thought.

One of many that seemed to haunt him lately.

Why had his sister even called? Ashley had this unrealistic view of their family, actually, of the world. She saw what she wanted to see. But life wasn't all hearts and flowers. And their family would never be like one on some TV sitcom. Did she really think if he came home, he and Mom would miraculously reconcile? Nothing could make him forget all the years she'd stood by and done nothing.

Nope. He'd only make things worse if he set foot in that house. If he even laid eyes on the old man, the one thing they would not be having was a reconciliation.

Making things worse seemed to be his thing lately. The way he'd left it with Gabby kept nagging at him. His fingers had hovered over his cell phone several times, but he'd checked the impulse to call her. What a stupid move *that* would've been. He shouldn't have even given his number to her. The woman was emotional C-4. He'd dodged a bullet.

Still, it wouldn't hurt to check in with his buddy later tonight. Make sure there weren't any snafus setting up the security system. Double-check that Neil had spared no expense. Then Clay could have a guilt-free Gabby memory dump and be free of her once and for all.

Shaking his head, he barely managed to get his fists back up in position without wincing, while the kid bounced from one foot to the other as if he could go a hundred more rounds. It made Clay feel way older than thirty.

Just as the kid came at him, glove swinging, Doughboy called to him, "Hey, Hounddog."

Clay glanced toward Doughboy and the kid's glove connected with his jaw. He staggered back, seeing stars.

Shaking off the dizziness, he rubbed his jaw. Was it sad that he was grateful for an excuse to stop? He lifted both arms to end the match, and then scowled at Doughboy as he removed his mouth guard. "What was so important?"

Doughboy smirked as he held up Clay's cell phone. "Your phone's buzzing."

"Catch you later, kid." He used his teeth to untie his right glove while he bent under the rope to leave the ring. Glove off, he grabbed his phone from Doughboy. Barrow had called? When a simple text to let him know he'd finished with the apartment would've done?

He headed for the locker room, pulling off his other glove with his teeth, and dialed his buddy.

"Barrow Security," Neil answered.

"Give me a sitrep."

"I'm here at Gabby's." Neil sounded dead serious.

Clay stilled. Was Gabby standing right there? Should he talk to her? Then he grimaced. What was this? Junior high? "What's going on?"

"This was no punk looking for electronics. Somebody has it in for her."

A cold fear snaked down Clay's spine. "Get her out of there."

"I tried. She won't leave."

"Then make her leave."

"She said she ran once and it didn't solve anything. And honestly, there's a better way to deal with this."

"Did you—?"

"Chill, bro. I've set up perimeter cameras, silent alarms and twenty-four-hour video monitoring to my company. I gave her a smart grid to control the lights, and I even programmed her a mobile app. Nobody's getting in without her and us knowing about it."

"That's not good enough."

A split second of silence was followed by "Buddy, you want her any safer, you better come up here and guard her yourself. Actually, that's not a bad—"

Clay heard what sounded like a muffled cry in the background. Everything in him went on alert. "What was that?"

"Hold on."

More muffled voices, pitched low. Gabby's voice was shaking. Clay wanted to snap his phone in two. He wanted to leap from cell tower to cell tower and be at her apartment *now*.

"Barrow, what the hell is going on?" he yelled into his phone.

Waiting seconds for Neil to come back to his phone felt like days, weeks. "You're not going to like this."

"Barrow, I swear, if you don't tell me right now—"

"She just received a threat via Snapchat. And I quote, 'Don't go to Switzerland, or what happened in Paraguay will end worse for you this time.' End quote. Evidently, she's attending some international conference next week."

Clay swore long and hard. "Call the police."

"Already on it. But you know this won't be a high priority for them. It'll take weeks to trace the IP address."

There weren't enough curse words. Clay gritted his teeth. Gabby must be terrified. She'd come to him for help and he'd sent her back into harm's way. It didn't make sense but he felt responsible for her now. He wanted to be the one there with her, to wrap his arms around her and protect her. Swear he'd kill anyone that dared hurt her. His hand shook as he held the phone. "How's she handling it?" If he knew Gabby she was trying to be strong.

"Pale, but putting a brave face on it. She's gone to the restroom. You know—" Neil lowered his voice. "She could be doing this to herself just to get attention."

"You think she arranged to have herself kidnapped in a foreign country and get a guy killed, too? She's not like that. I know her."

"You *know* her? Bro, how involved are you with this woman?"

"I'm not. I mean, I am, but it's not like that."

There was silence on the other end. But Clay heard Neil's unspoken question loud and clear. What was it like, then? Clay had no answer. All he knew was Gabby had come to him when she had no one else to turn to. She'd trusted him. And he wasn't going to let anything happen to her. Not on his watch. "Look, Barrow, all I'm saying is I trust my gut and my gut tells me she's in real trouble and I want to make sure she's safe."

Neil whistled. "You've got it bad."

Clay scoffed. "You're delusional. Just because I don't think she's a crackpot."

"So, what do you want to do? I have to be in Mumbai tomorrow."

What did he *want* to do? Or what *should* he do? Clay could barely think for all the rage and frustration raising his blood pressure. Surely Gabby wouldn't go to this conference now. On the other hand, he did have some leave coming…

No. He was no bodyguard. Better to convince Gabby to stay home.

But what if she wouldn't? And what if something happened to her and he wasn't there to stop it?

"Barrow, I want full background checks on everyone close to Gabby. Her family, her colleagues, even the bank president who was shot in the jungle. And send me a bill."

"You got it. And in the meantime?"

"I want to hire your best guy. I want someone watching her 24/7."

"No problem. I'll even give you the family discount. But, bro?"

"What?"

"Are you sure you don't want to take care of this yourself? I hear Switzerland can be a romantic getaway."

Clay cursed him and ended the call.

10

"THIS IS YOUR last chance to make the smart decision."

Ignoring Clay's warning—even if his low voice made her spine tingle—Gabby shouldered her phone at her ear while she handed her boarding pass to the Swiss Air Lines attendant.

"Gabby! Don't be stupid. It's not worth your life." Clay sounded really agitated now. He'd been trying all week to talk her out of attending the conference. Every night he called or texted to make sure she was safe. She had no clue how to feel about that. He'd made it clear when he dropped her off at the train in Virginia Beach that he didn't want to see her again. And things were so awkward between them whenever he contacted her.

She switched the phone to her other ear and grabbed the handle of her carry-on. "I appreciate your concern, Clay, I do. But I've been practicing my self-defense at a dojo and I have my pepper spray in my checked luggage." She swallowed a lump in her throat. "Thank you for everything, Clay. I have to go now."

Before he could say anything else, she clicked off the phone, dropped it in her purse and rolled her carry-on through the terminal door onto the jet bridge. But she stopped just on the other side.

Was she being stupid? He was right that once she got on this plane, there was no turning back. She reached for her Mary medal but, of course, it wasn't there. Panic paralyzed her. What good was a career if she was dead? What if she got kidnapped again? What if she died this time? Or what if someone else got killed because of her?

No. She closed her eyes. This was about more than her job. If she didn't get back on the horse now—or in this case, get on a plane—she'd never go anywhere again. Might as well move back in with her parents, join her mom cleaning houses and wait to die of old age. And darn it, she'd made a promise to herself in that jungle to have a life.

"Everything okay, Gabby?" James asked from behind her.

Startled, she moved to the side to let him and the other passengers go ahead. "I'm good," she answered, smiling at James. "Just making sure I didn't forget something."

Inhaling a deep breath, she hitched her purse up on her shoulder and headed down the jet bridge.

"Gabby! Wait!"

She looked back to see Clay lope up to the ticket agent and hand off a boarding pass. "Clay?"

Hefting a large black duffel over his shoulder, he caught up to her. "I'm going with you."

She couldn't believe he was here. He looked tense, grim, irritated. She made herself close her mouth. Then opened it again to refuse his offer. Well, not an offer so much as a command. But she felt safer having him beside her. She wasn't stupid. "What about the SEALs? How did you—"

"Can't a guy take some leave to be with his girl?" he cut her off as a few other passengers passed them by.

"His girl?"

He smiled, threw his arm around her shoulders, grabbed her carry-on with his free hand and propelled them down the jet bridge toward the plane. "We can't keep it a secret forever, you know. You'll have to tell everyone I'm your boyfriend eventually."

Boyfriend? She glanced at his hand as it squeezed her shoulder. Was it sad that knowing it was a ruse didn't keep her from relishing the sound of that?

For the entire flight, whenever anyone passed their seats, Clay grabbed her hand and held it, fingers entwined. Twice she woke up with her head on his shoulder. And once, she awoke with his hand caressing her cheek.

Or maybe he'd just been trying to move her.

Either way, nothing mattered—not twelve hours of traveling, nor the fact that it was the next morning local time yet felt like midnight to her, nor that once they arrived in Zurich they still had an hour train ride through the Alps to Lucerne. She was in Switzerland! With Clay posing as her boyfriend. To protect her.

Stepping off the train into the picturesque town square of Lucerne, with its medieval buildings and cobbled lanes, seemed like a fairy tale. And walking into the Hotel Palace Luzern with Clay's arm around her? She couldn't have even dreamed a fairy tale that good. The hotel used to be a real palace!

Their room had a balcony that overlooked the Reuss River. Gabby threw open the French doors and stepped out to the wrought-iron balustrade, huddling into her coat as she took in the view. Swans skimmed along the river's surface. White-tipped mountains jagged along the horizon, the tallest peaks hidden by clouds.

Her senses were overwhelmed. With nature. With the history here. With all the marble and gold in their opulent room.

With the giant bed dominating one wall.

Clay hadn't booked a separate accommodation, so... Was she really supposed to share a room with him for the next five days? He might be here to keep her body safe, but who was going to protect her heart? She was done throwing herself at him. But she hoped they could be friends. She guessed that was what he wanted.

Was it possible to mourn the loss of something she'd never even had?

"Keeping you safe here will be a nightmare." Clay spoke from behind her. "You don't go anywhere alone, got it?"

She turned to face him and found her nose almost touching his chest. It wasn't just the crisp air that made her want to snuggle closer to his heat. "You're going to attend the workshops with me?" She checked her conference program. "The Impact of Globalized Retrenchment on Risked Assets should be especially fascinating for you." She grinned up at him. How could she not? She was in Switzerland!

He didn't crack a smile. Not even a tiny lift of his lips. "How can you joke around?"

She sighed, sidestepped him and tugged off her coat. "I do realize the seriousness of my situation." Stopping in the middle of the room, she stretched out her arms and spun to face him. "But, come on, Clay. Look at this place. It's gorgeous. If I'm going to risk my life by being here, I might as well enjoy every minute. Carpe diem, right?"

He shook his head, his jaw working. He'd shaved the beard from last week, but after the long flight his five o'clock shadow was more like a day's growth. His mahogany hair was just long enough to have a slight wave. He looked so handsome, but so grim. She yearned to put her arms around him, hold him tight and assure him everything would be okay.

But he wouldn't appreciate that.

Looking closer, she could see tired lines around his eyes and between his brows. As far as she knew he hadn't slept on the flight over. "You must be exhausted. Why don't you take a nap? I promise I won't go anywhere without you."

He frowned while his gaze shifted from her to the bed. "I'm fine."

With a frustrated growl she rolled her eyes. What? Did he think she would jump him and demand sex if he let down his guard? She had her pride. "You can't protect me if you're falling asleep."

He shrugged out of his heavy coat. "I've been in war zones under heavy fire on less sleep than this."

"Oh. Right." She remembered he hadn't slept in the jungle that night either.

Expression stern, he stalked to the seating area, threw his coat over a chintz-covered chair and then paced to stand in front of a gilded seven-foot wardrobe. He flung open the doors and slid his hands along the wood panels and behind the television.

His muscles bunched beneath his sweater. Every move was a study in control and efficiency. She could watch him for hours.

But she wasn't into torturing herself. "I guess you've been to lots of exotic places around the world."

"I hate traveling." He glanced at her with a grimace then resumed his inspection of the room, running his hands over the dresser, yanking open every drawer.

"That's understandable. Guess there isn't much to see in the places you usually get sent to."

He prowled to a bedside table, lifted a lamp to inspect the base and then felt the shade.

She cleared her throat. "Not a lot of sights to see in a war zone." She should just stop.

Ignoring her, he stalked into the bathroom, opened the cabinet beneath the marble vanity, checked inside the shower stall.

Hoping he might tell her something—anything—about himself, she followed him to the bathroom. "Ever been anywhere that wasn't a war zone?"

He paused and met her gaze. "Sometimes we stop over for some R & R before returning stateside."

"Really? Like where?"

He leaned a hip on the vanity and folded his arms across his chest. "Germany. Japan. Guam." He shifted his gaze upward "Hawaii, Spain. Rio, once."

"Wow. You really have been everywhere. I'd never even left Texas until I moved to New York." She'd been twenty-four and never farther than three hours from home. "How long have you been in the Navy?"

"Joined when I was seventeen. So…thirteen years."

"I thought you had to be eighteen to join the military."

"My stepdad had to sign for me." A hard glint came into his eyes. "'Bout the only time he ever said yes to anything I wanted."

Sounded like there was no love lost between him and his stepdad. "What about your mom? Did she mind you joining the Navy so young?"

He shrugged. "Didn't seem to care one way or the other." He rummaged through the complimentary basket of shampoos and lotions next to the sink. "Never did."

Was he saying his mother never cared about him? That couldn't be right. But Gabby remembered he'd told her he went to work in a quarry when he was fourteen… "Are they still alive—your mom and dad?"

"Stepdad," he replied, his tone filled with bitterness. "And yes. As far as I know."

Whoa. As far as he knew? She flinched from his barely contained anger. "And your sister, is she married?"

"Unfortunately. Two cute kids, though."

"Her husband's not…nice?"

"Do you know anyone happily married? I mean, not including newlyweds?"

"Happily?" She thought about her parents. They weren't *un*happy. But they weren't giddy in love either. She knew they loved each other, but she'd never heard them actually say the words. She got the sense that they each did what was expected of them, played their part. They were a team. Was that enough for a happy marriage? Gabby swallowed a lump in her throat. She wanted more. "I guess not. But that doesn't mean—"

"And my buddy—" He snapped his fingers. "Oh yeah, you know Neil. He got engaged a few weeks ago." He shook his head. "Poor sap."

O-kay. Message received loud and clear. To Clay, marriage was a fate worse than death. His childhood must've been pretty bad. Yet he was a good man. He'd treated her with nothing but respect. And he'd made something of his life. Served his country. Now he was risking himself again for her. There was more to him than—what had he called himself at the embassy in Paraguay? A grunt? No, he was definitely more than that.

Part of her longed to make him see that two people who were truly in love could make a relationship work. Could be happy. But who was she kidding? The other part of her knew she wasn't the type of woman to inspire that kind of all-consuming love. She'd made enough of a fool of herself around this guy to last a lifetime.

Let it go, Gabby.

"Well, I'm taking a long soak in that fancy tub, then

ordering room service for dinner—since I have a per diem—and studying the conference schedule before bed." She spun and headed for her suitcase, kicked off her shoes and tore off her suit jacket.

While she removed her earrings, she caught Clay from the corner of her eye checking out the sofa, grabbing the extra blanket from the wardrobe, rearranging the cushions. Guess he was sleeping on the couch. With a sigh she grabbed her phone, the room service menu and her toiletries case, and headed for the bathroom.

As she sank into the huge tub of hot water and bubbles, she closed her eyes, laid her head back and tried not to imagine Clay sitting behind her, arms wrapped around her, nibbling on her neck...

HE MUST BE out of his mind to have used up the last of his leave for this.

When Clay heard water splashing on the other side of the bathroom door, he hightailed it for the hallway and positioned himself outside their room.

Five days of this. Five days of her eyes sparkling with excitement. Her brows crinkling in concern. Biting her lip.

How had she gotten him to talk about his mother and stepfather? He'd probably talked more about his family with her than...anyone. Even Neil.

He needed something to do to take his mind off Gabby.

Gabby lying naked in a bathtub...

A door opened down the hall and Clay straightened from the door, his hand reaching for the pistol under his left armpit. A couple stepped out, heads tilted toward each other, talking as they walked toward the elevator. He smiled and nodded as they passed.

How was he supposed to protect Gabby in this environment? He almost hadn't gotten his guns through airport security. And he still needed to do some recon of the area. Scope out the hotel's back exits and employee entrances. Talk with the chief of security and his team. Inform them of the situation. Ask for a detailed layout of the hotel...

Had he been in the hallway long enough for Gabby to have her bath? How much time did a woman take when she was soaking? He closed his eyes while he imagined her soaping her breasts, her nipples peeking just above the water...

The elevator dinged and the doors swished open. A hotel employee rolled out a room service cart with silver-domed plates. Clay kept his hand on his weapon as the guy stopped the cart in front of him. Why hadn't he told Gabby not to order room service? Should he taste all that food? There was a lot to being a bodyguard. Things he hadn't thought of that Neil would know. He should've hired one of Neil's men to do this.

He tipped the room service guy and assured him he'd wheel the cart into the room himself, and then watched the employee get on the elevator. After the doors closed behind the guy, Clay lifted all the lids— Gabby had ordered two of everything—and checked under the skirt of the rolling table, then used his keycard to get back inside the room.

The bathroom door was still shut, and he moved

closer to listen for signs that she might be done. "Gabby, dinner is here," he called through the door.

No answer.

He knocked. "Gabby, are you okay?"

Still no answer. No water splashing. He grabbed the doorknob. Locked. "Gabby! I'm coming in!"

Clay drew his firearm and shoved his shoulder into the bathroom door. As it slammed open, he burst into the room, Sig aimed.

Gabby screamed and straightened, dropping the foot she'd had propped on the edge of the tub. When she twisted to face him, her earbuds popped out as the phone they were attached to fell off the vanity. She stood frozen, wide-eyed terror etched on her face.

And every inch of her was beautifully, gorgeously naked.

11

CLAY HOLSTERED HIS Sig and curled his hands into fists. Only sheer will kept him from sweeping her into his arms and carrying her out to that big bed… Oh, the places his mind went as he absorbed every light and shadow playing over Gabby's golden-brown skin, her long, black hair curling in wet ringlets. He wanted to cup her full breasts and palm her bronze nipples until they tightened to hard pebbles he could flick with his tongue and—

He spun to face the door and somehow made it out onto the balcony. Deep breaths. Bracing cold air. What he really needed was to cannonball into the freezing river six stories below. His cock actually throbbed.

Once he'd gotten himself under control, he went back inside. Gabby was sitting at the table where she'd set out the food. She'd put on loose-fitting pajamas with a thick robe. He approached. Her hands shook as she stirred her tea. Her long black hair was still wet, but slicked back from her flushed face. Baggy flannel pj's had never looked so—the word that came to him was *alluring*.

He took a deep breath. "I knocked."

She winced. "Yes, I—I realize that now."

"I called your name. Three times."

"I'm sorry I scared you."

"For your own safety you have to be able to hear."

"You're right. I wasn't thinking." Her tone was apologetic, but her dark eyes, staring so candidly into his, not so much. They...wanted him.

No! He was only here for one reason, and he sure couldn't keep her safe with his pants down around his ankles. "I have to—check on some things."

"Now?"

He grabbed his coat, then turned back and pointed a finger at her. "Don't let anyone—I mean anyone—in this room. I have a key. From now on we'll use a code. I'll ask if you checked the weather and if you're safe, you say yes, if something's wrong you answer no, got it?"

She nodded.

By the time he returned to the room it was after eight. Gabby was asleep in the big bed. She'd left the bathroom light on, but he would've known her whereabouts by the mumbling. Clay smiled when she muttered something about term loans. Maybe she was composing her bank pun of the day.

He stripped down to his shorts, laid his Sig on the coffee table and fell onto the sofa. The conference started early tomorrow and he would need to be vigilant.

For now, he'd done all he could. The hotel manager

and security personnel had been alerted. He'd checked all the fire exits and employee entrances.

Sheets rustled on the bed and Gabby mumbled something as she turned. Clay closed his eyes, picturing her in sexy lingerie instead of the flannel pj's. Picturing her coming to him, peeling off panties, climbing over him… *Just stop.*

Could he take four more nights of this?

"ANALYZING CURRENT EVENTS Affecting International Financial Markets?" Clay read the sign on the easel in front of one of the meeting rooms. "This is something actual humans are interested in?"

Gabby blinked at the words, but all she could think about was seeing Clay emerge from the steamy bathroom this morning wearing only a pair of low-riding jeans, toweling his hair dry. She'd caught a glimpse of a couple of tattoos. One of an eagle wrapped in the American flag across the left side of his chest, another on his right upper arm of an anchor with the word *Navy* over it.

How was she going to concentrate on global markets when she could still picture water droplets trailing down his chest?

She stepped out of the way as other conference attendees filed into the room. "Well, lucky for you, you don't have to stay. What are you going to do with your free time?"

He seemed taken aback. "What do you think? I'll be waiting right here. I go where you go."

"Oh." Right. He was here as her bodyguard. Of

course, she knew that. "I don't think a real boyfriend would—"

His gaze darted behind her, and then he cupped her jaw in one hand and covered her mouth with his.

It took only a moment for her to stop resisting and melt into his kiss. She couldn't prevent a little moan of desire as he moved his lips over hers, languorously, thoroughly...then it was over.

She opened her eyes as cool air replaced the warmth of Clay's mouth.

A throat cleared beside her. "Want to introduce me, Gabby?" James looked at her expectantly and then at Clay.

Her cheeks heated in embarrassment. PDAs were unprofessional. And especially in front of James. When, less than two weeks ago, she'd been on a date with him. What must he think of her? Then she realized: she didn't care what James thought. About anything.

Clay returned James's stare through narrowed eyes. "Clay Bellamy." He extended his right hand.

"James Pender." He shook Clay's hand, obviously not recognizing him from the rescue in Paraguay.

Clay put one arm around her shoulders and gazed warmly into her eyes. "I couldn't stand being away from Gabby for a whole week, so I bought a ticket at the last minute and surprised her at the airport." He stared at James pointedly, even raising a supercilious eyebrow.

James's right eye twitched, and then he gave a forced smile. "Well, I'll see you in there, Gabby." He nodded and then strolled inside.

"What is it about that guy?" Clay stared after him.

"James?"

"His background check was clear. Still, there's something..."

Gabby studied James's retreating figure. "But he was kidnapped, too. And he was mugged with me, as well."

"What?" Clay let go of her shoulder and turned to face her. "You never mentioned he was with you when you were mugged."

"I didn't think it was relevant."

After scrutinizing her for a few seconds, Clay shrugged. "Maybe it isn't." He brushed his lips overs hers. "Have a good day, sweetheart." Then he moved behind a marble pillar across the hall and took out his phone.

Gabby resisted the urge to bring her fingers to her lips and headed into the room. *Sweetheart?* How was she supposed to concentrate now? All she wanted to do—all she seemed capable of doing—was reliving the feeling of Clay's lips on hers. Of his strong hand framing her face. Of spending the rest of the week as his girlfriend.

CLAY PULLED UP a game on his phone and leaned against the pillar outside the meeting room. Something wasn't adding up. Neil hadn't uncovered anything unusual about Gabby's coworkers. If it hadn't been for the Snapchat threat, Clay could've passed off the mugging, and even the break-in, as coincidence, and the Paraguay kidnapping as exactly what it seemed: criminals motivated by money, with Gabby just a random victim.

And even though the kidnapping in Paraguay hadn't happened until after the last day of the conference, he couldn't assume the perp would wait this time. Whether the incidents were related or not, until he knew otherwise, the threat was real. And Gabby's safety was his first priority.

Gabby.

In her boxy, dark suit and hair pulled back in a plain ponytail, she didn't look like a seductress. But he'd still wanted her. With her lips still glistening from his kiss, she'd looked at him with that soft expression in her eyes. Made him feel like a somebody. He wanted to box up that feeling and stick it in his pocket. Keep it with him always.

He winced, thinking about that kiss. It could be said that he was taking this boyfriend act a tad too far. But he had to be convincing, otherwise Gabby would be in jeopardy. Still, if she seemed vulnerable, maybe it would flush the stalker out. No. No way. It was a risk he refused to take.

Right.

If he was being honest though, Gabby was a financial whiz, and surrounded by all these brain trust types, he'd thought a kiss might remind her that he was more than a glorified watchdog. Shaking his head at his own unbelievable absurdity, Clay shot a quick text to Neil, and then settled in to do what he'd come here for: keeping Gabby safe.

DURING THE NEXT couple of days, Gabby's ability to focus only worsened. Clay followed her from workshop to workshop, holding her hand, touching her arm or her shoulder, brushing his lips against her cheek or temple—though he didn't kiss her on the mouth again. He would smile down at her as if he was lost in love. How was she supposed to concentrate on the keynote speech at lunch when Clay sat so close, his arm draped around her, his masculine scent driving her wild?

But the nights were the most unbearable. After having him so near all day, to have him turn cold and distant once they entered their room seemed especially cruel. She kept to the bed, going over her notes from the day, while he stayed in the sitting area, mostly on his phone, or checking his gun. She couldn't take much more.

When she emerged from the bathroom in her pajamas and robe, he'd already turned off the lights, but there was enough ambient light through the French doors for her to make out the shadows.

He lay silently on the sofa. But she knew he wasn't asleep. He was too still. Too quiet. He had this way of being absolutely motionless, yet powerfully alert. He had one hand behind his head, one knee bent. The blanket pulled only to his waist, so she had an eyeful of wide shoulders, broad chest and huge biceps.

Intensely aware of him, she took off her robe, crawled into bed. She touched her bare throat out of habit while saying her prayers and felt the loss of her medal acutely. She could sure use Abuelita's advice right now.

It'd been three days and not one sign of trouble. She'd received no more threats. She felt as if she'd caused a lot of inconvenience for nothing. "Clay?"

"Yeah?" he answered quickly, as if he'd been waiting for her to say something.

"I—I think maybe the threat was a joke. Or... someone trying to scare me into not coming here. But when whoever it was realized it didn't work, and you were here with me. Maybe there is no danger. Maybe you wasted your vacation time."

"Don't worry about it. It was my decision."

"But you've been cooped up in the hotel all week. Don't you want to ride the funicular up to the Alps, walk through the glacier tunnel, sit in a tavern and taste the *chögelipastetli*?"

"What the heck is chew-goalee-paste-Italy?"

She giggled. "The travel guide says it's veal dumplings in a pastry shell. Or there's cordon bleu, or fondue—"

"I'm good." His voice sounded strained.

"But—"

"*No*, we Charlie Mike."

"What?"

"Charlie Mike. We continue the mission. Now go to sleep."

Continue the mission? She was just another job to him. She shook her head. Of course she was.

She bit her lip and turned over, punching the pillow into shape. She closed her eyes and tried to think of the workshops she wanted to attend the next day and the formal dinner tomorrow night to mark the close of the conference. Now she wished she'd bought a new gown for the event. Something sexy that would've made Clay look twice. Maybe three times.

And *why* was she still thinking things like that?

She turned over on her other side, restless, aroused.
She could hear him breathing, so close by. She was
tempted to get up and go over to that sofa and—no.
She couldn't. She flopped onto her back.

Clay cursed. "I swear, Gabriella, can't you just be
still?" He threw back the blanket, strode over to the
French doors and ran a hand through his hair. "You're
driving me crazy."

Stung, she jackknifed up in the bed, folding her arms
across her chest. "Feel free to get your own room. Or
better yet, go home."

He spun and stalked to her bedside, hands low on
his hips. "Maybe I should."

She pushed up to her knees and shoved him in the
chest. "Then go!"

He barely budged, but with his jaw set, his nostrils
flared.

What had she done?

Chest heaving, he scowled at her.

"I'm sorry. I—"

He caught the back of her head in one hand and
claimed her mouth with his.

She moaned, threw her arms around his neck and
poured all her bottled-up passion into the kiss. He
matched her passion, moving his lips over hers. He
kissed along her neck, and she rubbed her cheek against
his rough jaw. Then his mouth was back on hers, desperate, possessive.

He wrenched away, eyes closed. "I can't do this."

She trailed her lips down to his collarbone while her

hands caressed his pecs. "We're safe here. Just for tonight." She opened her mouth and lightly bit his nipple.

"Gabby." He clasped her head between his hands, but he didn't stop her. So she pressed kisses to his taut stomach.

"Don't you want—" He sucked in a quick breath when she stuck her tongue in his belly button. "To wait?"

"No. I don't want to wait one..." She kept kissing him, even lower. "More." Lower. "Second." She got to the waistband of his jeans and started unbuttoning, but he grabbed her hands.

"I mean, wait for marriage."

She stilled. Marriage? To the guy who'd acted as if he'd rather be shot than get married? She sat back on her heels. "You want to get married?" She might be falling in love, but she wasn't ready for—

"Heck, no. Not me. Just...in general. Someday."

Wait a minute. She was falling in love? And, "in general"? What did that mean? "Why would I—?"

"In the jungle that night. You told me you'd never..." Oh.

She squirmed. "So, because I— You think that I'm, like, saving myself?"

He splayed his hands low on his hips and dropped his chin, exhaling a deep breath. "Why else would—"

"Lots of reasons." Reasons she didn't care to explain. "Look, I'm not—" she folded her arms and grimaced "—saving myself, okay? I have a career, things I want to experience, a life I want to live. I'm not ready to be tied down any more than you are." Exasperated, embarrassed, she moved to get around him and crawl off the bed. "I just—I thought—"

"Wait." He grabbed her shoulders and she looked up into his serious face. He bent and she rose up on her knees again, their mouths meeting to taste, to explore. His mouth was magic. He pressed her hips against the hardness behind his zipper. Her arms snaked around his neck again.

With a soft whimper, she fell back and he followed her down onto the bed, kissing her collarbone while he worked the buttons of her pajama top. She wanted to unbutton his jeans but she was too busy running her hands over his bare back and chest.

His muscles rippled beneath her palms as he spread her top open and lowered his head to her breast. His lips closed around one nipple and sent a sweet, tantalizing ache straight to her core. She held him and tried not to cry out as he licked and then suckled first one breast and then the other.

Pajamas. Needed. Off. She struggled to get her arms out of the sleeves and then wiggle free of the bottoms. As she kicked them away he lifted his hips, undid his jeans and stripped out of them. He left her, but only for a second and only for a packet he pulled from his duffel. Then he settled back between her thighs, and returned his attention to her breasts.

The room was too dark. She wanted to *see* him. See it. She'd gotten only a brief glimpse of narrow waist and flat stomach and a long shadow jutting up from darker curls. But there'd be time later for exploration. For now she'd be happy with just feeling him. And feel him she did. His hard length rubbed against the place she needed him most as he rocked his hips and brought his mouth back to hers.

His kisses had a frantic quality as he fumbled with the packet, then reached between them to rub his fingers between her folds. He groaned.

Was that a bad thing? But he didn't sound as if it was a bad thing. He slipped a finger inside her and it felt so glorious she lifted her hips. She told him, "More. You." Geez, she'd been reduced to monosyllables.

He smiled against her lips and slowly guided himself to her entrance, rubbing his penis against her. "Do I need to...go slow?"

"What?" She kissed his jawline.

He lifted his head to look her in the eyes. "You know, be careful?"

"Oh. You mean—" Could she be any more embarrassed? "No. Uh, not any more than you would usually, I don't think." He was sweet to ask, but what did she know?

With a nod, he pressed slowly inside, watching her as if she might cry out in pain. But she smiled her encouragement and he didn't stop until he was seated to the hilt.

It felt nothing like how she'd imagined. There was a fullness, yes, a stretching. He was large. But it didn't hurt. She'd been more than ready. She studied his face, which had hardened to granite, his eyes squeezed shut. Then he started to pull out, but she locked her ankles around his flanks.

"Where are you going?"

"Gabby, I'm not going anywhere." His voice was a steely rasp. He pierced her with a look. "I need to move."

"Right." She knew that. Feeling foolish, she dropped her feet to either side of him and he slid almost all the way out and then pushed back in.

Oh, yes, that was—he did it again. And again. Relentless. The friction created a rising pleasure. He'd lowered to his elbows, his chest against hers, so close she thought she could feel his heartbeat. The intimacy was almost too much. She had to hold back her emotions.

He swiped a strand of hair from her face and kissed her as he rocked harder and faster until he'd set up a rhythm that sent her spiraling. As he chanted her name, his arms slipped underneath her and he nuzzled her neck. His pace never wavering.

She wanted to hold him like this forever. She wanted to believe he felt the same way. Being with him, like this, would have to be enough. It was *the* moment and she was in it. Finally. Gripping his shoulders, she moaned and bucked and reached a pinnacle. She cried out, unable to stop herself. She clung to him until her breathing slowed and a languidness overtook her. Then she realized he'd stilled.

He was watching her with a look of wonder. "You're beautiful."

That was when she definitely fell in love.

12

EVENTUALLY HE'D HAVE to go cold turkey, break this need he had, this craving for Gabby to look at him that way. As if he was her very own hero. His brain—what was left of it—knew that she had nothing to compare him to, but his ego was telling him he was a genius at sex.

And speaking of... He was still rock hard and aching. But he'd wanted to watch her without being caught up in his own pleasure, so he'd held off. He'd never done that before. Of course, he'd never been anyone's first before either.

Gabby closed her eyes and sighed.

"You okay?"

Her eyes flew open. "Can we...Charlie Mike?"

He huffed. "I'll never think of continuing the mission in the same way again." He rolled to his back and took her with him. "How about you ride me this time?"

With a wicked grin, she leaned forward to flatten her palms on his chest. "Like this?" She rose up and then slowly sank onto him.

His hands went to her hips, then he slid them up to cup her breasts. "That works."

She rose and sank again. Faster, experimenting with different angles. Between the impish gleam in her eyes and his hands full of soft luscious breasts, he lost control. He groaned and couldn't keep from lifting his hips to thrust into her. Every muscle strained. Breathing ceased, vision blurred, sounds faded as his mind and body seized.

But she was still riding him, and every movement rocked him with aftershocks until he had to beg her to stop. Or, at least, it felt like begging. What he actually said was "Okay. Okay." He couldn't manage anything more coherent than that.

He curled an arm around her and pulled her against him. She laid her cheek on his chest, still breathing as hard as he was. He liked her breasts cushioned on him. Liked her fingers stroking through the hair at his temple. Liked how he fit perfectly around her body.

She drew in a deep breath and let it out on a long humming sigh. "Wow. That was…" She sighed again. "I minored in English and I got nothing but clichés right now."

Clay chuckled. "You're good at math *and* English? Is there anything you're not good at?"

"I know what *you're* good at." She grinned, and then dropped kisses onto his chest.

He scoffed. "You just don't have anything to compare it to."

She stiffened in his arms.

"Okay, that didn't come out right. I've had plenty to compare it to and yeah, this was…" He inwardly winced to admit how awesome it had felt. "More than good."

She lifted her head and offered him a guardedly hopeful look. "Really?"

Something in his chest twisted at that expression. This conversation seemed to be going where he didn't want it to go. He raised a mocking brow. "Yes, I really have had plenty to compare it to."

Her eyes narrowed. "Never mind." She tried to sit up.

He tightened his hold around her. No more teasing. This was her first time and he guessed she was worried about her performance. But she had nothing to worry about. He put a finger under her chin to raise her gaze to his. "The truth?" He looked her straight in the eye. "You were amazing."

She studied him a moment, as if gauging whether to believe him or not, then she reached up to peck him on the mouth and vaulted off the bed.

"Where are you going?" He turned to watch her, spying the scar on her midback from where the bullet had grazed her. The sight brought up a powerful urge to go back to Paraguay and beat those kidnappers to a pulp.

"I just can't lie still right now." Throwing him a half-hearted smile, she reached for her robe and strolled out onto the balcony.

He laid there a moment. She was the most unpredictable woman he'd ever met. What was going through that brilliant mind of hers? He didn't want to even think about the enormity of what he'd just done. What *they'd* just done. Or, maybe it wasn't that big of a deal to her.

That was a depressing thought.

Shaking his head, he got up and padded to the bathroom to clean himself up, then stepped into his shorts before joining her on the balcony. The snowcapped mountains glowed from the lights of the city. Below them, he could hear the rushing current of the river. The town square was mostly empty, quiet. The world seemed like a peaceful place from here.

Like with women, appearances could be deceiving. She shivered and drew the robe tighter.

"It's pretty cold out here." He put his arm around her shoulders and curled her into his chest. "Probably ought to get some sleep." He brought his nose to the top of her head, noting the intoxicating fragrance of her hair.

"You go ahead. I'll be in in a minute."

Did she want to talk? Was she regretting losing her virginity to him? Surely she wasn't expecting professions of love.

He put his other arm around her and rubbed her back. "No way I'm leaving you out here alone."

She didn't speak for a long while, and then "You really think someone's after me? I'm starting to wonder if it wasn't just a sick prank."

He drew in a deep breath and gently rested his chin on top of her head. "Until we know otherwise we treat it as real."

"I guess the question is, why me?"

"Something to do with work? A coworker, maybe? Neil said the perp has some serious anger issues. Anyone you can think of who might have a grudge? Anyone been passed over for a promotion? Seem to resent you for any reason?"

She shook her head against his chest. "No. I've only been there two years."

"Probably someone who can hack into personnel files, since they found out where you live."

"That could be anyone." She brought her hand up to her throat.

"Come on. Come back to bed with me." Without giving her time to object, he steered her inside, closed the French doors and guided her into the bed. Before he gave it any thought he crawled in beside her under the thick comforter and drew her into his arms.

Snuggling against him, she circled his waist with her free arm and drew a knee up between his thighs. Her feet were icy. Though she wore the robe, and he still had on his shorts, lying like this felt more intimate than when he'd been inside her.

"I wish I hadn't lost my Mary medal," she murmured.

He vaguely recalled, back in Virginia Beach, her mentioning a medal. "The one you lost during the mugging?"

"It was the most special thing I owned. My grandmother died not long after she gave it to me, and I've always thought of it as my connection to her. A way of talking to her. And—"

When she didn't continue, he prompted, "And?"

"It sounds really superstitious when I say it out loud."

He chuckled. "Nobody's more superstitious than a sailor."

He felt her smile. "Really? What are Navy guys superstitious about?"

"Everything. We throw a few coins in the ocean

before a voyage to appease Neptune. Never—I mean never—wash a coffee mug on board ship or you'll have bad weather. And you know that candy that comes in the MRE? We throw it out. Some guys believe if you eat it on a mission you won't come back alive."

She pulled away and looked into his eyes. "Okay, I don't feel so crazy now." Her smile flashed in the dim room, her brown eyes crinkled. "I mean, I can't blame them. Why tempt fate, right?"

"Darn straight. Better safe than sorry."

Her smile faded. "I will always pray that you come back safe from your missions."

Clay had to swallow a sudden lump in his throat. He doubted anyone had ever hoped for his safe return. And he'd made sure to keep it that way. "Thank you. That means a lot." Then he gave her a big grin. "Tell me about your medal."

Her hand pressed against her throat. "Sometimes I think it's her way of talking to me. When I touch it, I can hear her voice in my head giving me her wisdom, or reassurance."

"But you don't hear her voice anymore since you lost it?"

She tilted her head, wondering. Then her smile flashed again. "You know? I do still feel her presence." She bent to give him a kiss on the mouth. "Thank you for helping me realize that." With a dreamy grin she lay beside him and started caressing his chest, circling her finger around his nipple. "What about you?"

"Hmm?" he grunted, occupied with what she was doing to him and how it was affecting his cock.

"Are your grandparents still alive?"

"Don't know."

She froze midswirl and shot him a look of incredulity. "How can you not know?"

He shrugged. "My mother's parents disowned her when she got pregnant with me. And my dad split when I was still a baby, so I never met his parents."

"But didn't you mention a stepfather? What about his mom and dad?"

"Never met them either."

She frowned at him.

The last thing he wanted to talk about was his family. Feeling a bit smug, he grabbed her hand and slid it down to encircle his growing erection. "Can't we find something better to talk about?"

"Mmm." She jumped up and switched on the bedside lamp, then returned to peel off his shorts. "I want to see what it looks like."

She'd never seen a penis before? Clay rose up on his elbows to watch her. "Okay." Was that what tonight was about for her? One more new experience to cross off her list? And he just happened to be around at the right time?

And why should that bother him? So what if she was using him? It's not like he would want anything more.

She stroked and played with him, running a finger down its length and back again, rubbing the head and along the rim. The more she studied it, the longer and harder it grew. He couldn't help smiling at her curiosity.

Then she licked it and he quit smiling. She cupped his balls and stroked him. When she glanced up for his reaction he tried to give her a look of pleased encouragement, but it was probably more like a goofy grin. When she took the whole thing in her mouth, he groaned. His head fell back and his hips lifted as she used her sweet tongue to bring him to the brink.

"Gabby." He said her name on a gasp and stilled her with a palm to her cheek. "Wait."

"No, I want to watch you—it. Can I?"

"In a minute. First, it's your turn."

GABBY KNEW WHAT was coming—or she hoped she did—and she wasn't sure how she felt about it. A dozen thoughts flitted through her mind. Fat thighs. Waxed enough? Embarrassing? Awkward. Then Clay was untying her robe and sliding it down her shoulders, placing kisses on the skin he revealed, pulling the sleeves off, more soft kisses on her jaw, behind her ear.

Before she knew it she was naked and lying on her back and Clay was kissing her breasts, her stomach and then…there. If ever there was a time to marvel at her luck it was now, so she freed her mind and arched her back. His tongue was doing the most exquisite things to her clitoris. And the things he did with his lips and sometimes, very gently, his teeth. And when he brought his fingers into play, she traveled beyond consciousness to a place where only pleasure existed.

She wasn't sure how many times she'd come when she heard the crinkling of a packet and then felt him crawl between her thighs and slip inside. He called her name from far away and she opened her eyes to see him smiling at her.

"There you are. Thought I lost you for a minute."

Using her shoulder to wipe the tear off her cheek, she threw her arms around his neck and kissed his throat. *I love you.* She had to clamp her mouth shut to keep from saying it out loud. He wouldn't want to hear it. He'd think she was presuming, or he'd tell her it was just because he'd rescued her and was protecting her like he had in the jungle.

And who knows, maybe he was right. She couldn't be objective about it, could she? That was the nature of falling in love. Or, at least, infatuation. No. Better to enjoy this night—and maybe tomorrow night if she was lucky, and then let him go.

He pumped into her. "Hey."

She drew back to look at him. "Hmm?"

"Still with me?" He moved in her again and she felt the pleasurable ache, but lethargy was setting in. She was so relaxed.

"Mmm-hmm." She held on tight to his shoulders.

"How about we let you watch next time, okay?"

She nodded. "Okay."

He thrust one last time and threw his head back. A vein stood out in his neck while he gritted his teeth. Then he was gathering her into his arms and turning her onto her side and pulling the covers up to her chin.

"Thank you," she thought she'd mumbled, but maybe not. All she knew was his warm body was snuggled beside her and his hand came around her to cup a breast, and she was happier than she'd ever been.

13

THE NEXT MORNING Gabby smiled before she even opened her eyes. She couldn't remember when she'd slept so deeply. Still groggy, she opened one bleary eye at a time and pushed the hair out of her face. She rolled to the middle of the bed.

Nothing but cold sheets.

What had she expected? That she'd wake up in Clay's arms and he'd smile and tell her he loved her? Yeah, and then they'd ride off on a white horse into the sunset. *Your life is not a telenovela, Gabriella Diaz.*

Tempted as she was to burrow back under the covers and hibernate, today was the last day of the conference and she had workshops to attend. She threw off the blankets and sat up. And blinked.

Clay, wearing only a pair of dark sweatpants with the word *Navy* in white letters down one side, his torso slick with a sheen of sweat, was doing push-ups on the floor at the foot of the bed.

She allowed herself a minute to watch him, admiring his bulging muscles and taut skin. The large tattoos added a dangerous maleness to his already tough persona. Then she hauled herself out of bed, grabbing her robe. She wanted to bend over and kiss his cheek, but he was concentrating on his workout, so she settled for a greeting. "Good morning."

His jaw tightened and he grunted.

Okay, he was probably trying to count. She wasn't a whiny baby, demanding his attention every second. She left him to it, and hopped in the shower. Maybe he'd join her.

But he didn't. By the time she got out of the shower, wrapped a towel around herself and dried her hair, he'd donned a sweatshirt and was sitting at the table drinking coffee.

"Mmm, coffee smells good." She smiled, pouring a cup for herself before taking the chair opposite him.

He stared at her, his gaze intense, and then it shifted away. "Can you put on some clothes, please?"

No "I had a great time last night." Not even a "How'd you sleep?" Gabby gathered the giant bath towel closer to her. She'd purposely not gotten dressed in the hopes that they might…Charlie Mike. But maybe, despite what he'd said last night, it hadn't been as wonderful for him as it had been for her. Maybe he hadn't wanted to hurt her feelings. Or maybe something else was bothering him.

Good relationships—not that they had a relationship, not a romantic one, anyway—but a professional one… What had she been thinking? Oh yeah, communication. Successful relationships were all about communicating well. "What's wrong?"

He scowled. "Nothing. You done in there?" He gestured toward the bathroom, brows raised.

So much for communicating. "Nothing? Clay, clearly something's wrong." She reached out and put her hand on his arm. "What's happened? Have you learned something about my situation I should know?"

"No." Scooting back, he got to his feet and spun, rubbing the back of his neck.

She folded her arms and waited.

He swung back to face her. "Are you okay?"

"Me? I'm fine. More than fine. I'm great." She grinned, hoping to tease him into a better mood. But he only nodded, seemingly lost in thought.

Tilting her head, she rolled her lips inward. "Clay, please talk to me."

"Look." He ran a hand through his hair, clearly exasperated. "I don't do cuddly morning afters, okay? I don't even usually do overnights. I'm not that kind of guy."

Gabby blinked. Well. He couldn't make himself any clearer than that. Turned out Clay was a very good communicator.

He grimaced. "I'll be ready to go in thirty." He strode into the bathroom, shut the door, and seconds later she heard the water turn on.

Wow. Her eyes stung with tears. Why should she cry? She'd known it was just sex for him.

The thing was, last night it hadn't felt like just sex. But without any other experiences with this, how would

she know? What she'd thought was an emotional connection had obviously been only in her own fevered
brain. But it wasn't as if she'd fallen all over the guy
this morning expecting a marriage proposal, geez. She
flung her towel over a chair and snatched a shirt and
pants off a hanger in the wardrobe.

Forget it. Last night was a special memory she'd
hold in her heart forever. But this morning she had
workshops to—

You know what? No. She'd decided not to take
life for granted anymore, hadn't she? And here she
was in another country! Maybe she'd play hooky and
take that funicular up to the peak of the mountain and
walk through that glacier tunnel. At the very least, she
wanted to cross that old, thatch-covered bridge span-
ning the Reuss, eat at that famous restaurant and see
the lion monument carved in stone. Buy souvenirs for
her family. Maybe even look for something beautiful to
wear tonight. She was going to enjoy her last day here.

But how could she enjoy it with Clay scowling at
her all day?

How irresponsible would it be to go off without
him? Right now, Gabby did not care. She had her pepper spray in her purse. She'd been practicing her self-
defense moves. And she was only going as far as the
shop in the hotel.

Without another thought, she dressed, threw her hair
in a ponytail and sent Clay a quick text telling him she
was going to the lobby. Then she headed downstairs.
There was a dress shop on the mezzanine level…

Striding defiantly out of the dress shop fifteen minutes later—and hundreds of dollars poorer—she almost knocked over James.

"Whoa!" He grabbed her upper arms. "Gabby."

"James." Here was someone who liked her. Someone who actually wanted to be with her.

"You okay?" James dropped his hands and stuck them in his pockets. "Aren't you supposed to be in a workshop in a few minutes?"

"Uh, yeah." She draped the bag with her dress over her arm. "I was just shopping while I waited for Clay."

James smoothed his hair off to the side with his opposite hand. "You two, that sure happened fast."

Guilt swamped her. "You know, I was thinking of skipping the workshops today. Maybe go eat fondue." She didn't have her coat, but, who cared? It was fairly mild today. "Want to come with?"

IN A CRAPPY MOOD, Clay stepped out of the shower and wiped the steam off the mirror. He took his razor and lathered up his jaw. Then he just stood there staring at himself. What an idiot. *Real smooth, Bellamy.* What was his problem? The bit about not doing cuddly mornings after? Kind of true. But who was he kidding? Last night things had been too…he didn't know. Just too everything.

Still, he owed Gabby an apology.

After he finished shaving, he zipped up his jeans, and swung open the bathroom door. "Listen, I'm really sorr—" The room was empty. "Gabby?" Frowning, he strode to the French doors and threw them open, even though he could see she wasn't out there. But she wouldn't—no *way* she would've left the room without him.

Grabbing his phone, he saw he had a text. From over forty-five minutes ago!

Lobby? Spewing every curse word he knew, he finished dressing and then raced downstairs. She was in so much trouble. Wait until he got his hands on her. What part of "don't go anywhere without me" did she not understand?

She was nowhere in the lobby. He checked the workshop rooms, scanning every one. He spoke with the hotel manager and security team. They hadn't seen her, but promised to notify him if they did. As soon as he made sure she was safe he was going to make her sorry.

His phone vibrated and he snatched it from his pocket.

At the Old Swiss House

She'd left the hotel? Pushing down a flare of panic, he got directions from the concierge and tried to control his temper all the way across the cobbled stones of the town square to the medieval building on the corner.

It wasn't until he yanked open the centuries-old door and everyone in the place stopped to stare at him that he realized he needed to calm down. He uncurled his fists, flexed them and tried to relax his face as he scanned the tables.

There. Sitting next to—that sniveling creep. She'd left the hotel to go out with *that* guy? She was staring at him, her expression a mixture of defiance and fear. She ought to be afraid.

He stalked over. "What do you think you're doing?"

She pasted on a smile and lifted a long-handled, two-pronged fork from a pot in the middle of the table. Slowly, deliberately, she lowered the melting, cheese-covered food into her mouth.

It might have been the most erotic thing he'd ever seen. Especially since she moaned as she chewed. The same moan she'd given him last night while something else had entered those luscious lips.

"James and I were discussing the Large Hadron Collider," she said after swallowing the cheese. "It's not far outside Geneva. I looked it up and we can be there in less than two hours by train, and they let visitors tour for free. Want to join us?"

Us? He needed to get his breathing under control. He wanted to smash something, preferably James's face. "No."

She shrugged. "Okay." Piercing another vegetable with the fork, she dipped it into the pot and swirled it around.

"And you're not going either."

Gabby shot him a menacing glare. "But, sweetheart," she intoned the words in a singsong voice. "It's the world's most powerful *particle collider.* The largest single machine in the world. Over ten thousand scientists and engineers from over a hundred countries collaborate in a tunnel a hundred and seventy-five meters deep. I'll never get another chance to see it." The last part was said through gritted teeth.

How did she spout all that information without even looking at her phone? If he needed another reason why he shouldn't be with her, then that was it. She had a brilliant mind. She was going places. He was only good for heavy lifting. Clay looked at James. "You mind giving us a minute?"

The guy cleared his throat and looked to Gabby, questioning. Clay wanted to haul him out of his chair and march him out the door by his collar.

Instead, Gabby pushed her chair back and stood, putting a hand on James's arm. "You go ahead and eat. I'll be right back." Her smile dropped when she shifted her gaze to Clay. "Outside?"

Clay took her arm, but she subtly pulled it out of his grasp. She stalked ahead of him, out the door and didn't stop until they were around the corner. Then she spun on him, arms crossed. "Yes?" There was that fake smile again.

"What the hell do you think you're doing leaving the room without me?"

"I decided back in that jungle in Paraguay that I was going to live a more purposeful life. I was going to be brave. If I wanted to stay cooped up somewhere, I wouldn't have come to Switzerland to begin with."

Clay bit the inside of his cheek "All you had to do was ask me first."

"I don't need your permission! And anyway, I'm not alone, I'm with James."

"Yeah, right," he mocked. "For all you know, that coward could be behind this threat."

She scoffed. "I told you, he was mugged that night, as well. Do you think he mugged himself?"

"It's possible he hired someone."

She blinked at that, but then shook her head. "Then why hasn't he done something this week? Or now? Besides, I have my pepper spray in my purse."

"You can argue all you want, but you don't go anywhere without me again. And I don't know about that collision thing. I'll look into the security situation there."

"I don't need your permi—" Her lips clamped and her eyes gradually lost their defiant spark. "Fine. But I really want to go. And we're leaving for home tomorrow."

He forced himself to relax. "If it's safe, we'll go."

"If we don't catch the next train we won't be back in time for the dinner tonight."

Her voice cracked and in that moment he would've done anything for her. "I'll start looking into it." He pulled out his phone. "But no James."

Her mouth fell open. "I can't tell him he can't go."

"I can."

Her mouth snapped shut and she cut him a look. "Fine. But I don't think I can get my fondue to go and it was really good." She stomped around him and headed into the restaurant.

And just like that their quarrel was over. Clay stared after her, watching her butt. He was shocked to realize he'd never actually argued with a woman before. How could he be furious and turned on at the same time? This was why he would never be in a relationship. Relationships were messy and complicated, and aggravating and *definitely* not worth the trouble. One minute she was angry and endangering herself with a stupid move, the next she was using common sense and giving in. In combat he knew who the enemy was. He knew what the mission was, and how to execute it. But how was he supposed to deal with her when she made him want to put her over his knee and spank her and, at the same time, pull her into his arms and kiss her senseless?

14

"I CAN'T BELIEVE we got into the guided tour!" Gabby stood on the train platform practically jumping with exhilaration from seeing the Large Hadron Collider. "And the Microcosm exhibition? I mean, wow. I wish we had time for the Universe of Particles exhibition, too. Just think of all the scientific advances waiting to be discovered. It's so exciting."

Clay stood beside her, arms folded, scanning the station like a...well, like a bodyguard. "You really get into all this stuff, don't you?"

She cringed. *Flying your nerd flag pretty high, there, Gabby.* She had been gushing about the applications in physics and technology for a while now. She'd pretty much babbled all morning to fill the silence. He hadn't acted bored during the tour, but he hadn't exactly acted interested either. "I told you I was a nerd."

He shrugged and turned his back to her. Great. Another one-sided conversation. He'd barely spoken to her at all. She supposed he was still mad about earlier, when she left the hotel without him.

Her hungry gaze roamed over his body. The wide shoulders. His narrow waist. And now she knew what it felt like. To lie next to his strong, solid heat. To run her hands over his firm flesh with its scars and chest hair. To have him hard and pulsing inside her... She sighed, dragging in a deep breath.

She'd wanted him all day. Even when he'd acted so rude this morning. Even when she was absorbed in watching the particle collider, she'd been aware of him standing next to her, aware of her body longing for his.

She swallowed. "Clay?"

He faced her, brows raised.

"I'm really sorry I left the room without you. It was colossally stupid. You came all this way just to protect me, and then I make things even more difficult for you by—"

"Forget it." He shook his head.

"It's no excuse, I know, but ever since the kidnapping I've been making some bad decisions."

His gaze riveted to her. "Was last night one of them?"

She frowned, wishing she knew what was going on in that mind of his. But she made sure she deliberately held his gaze. "I will *never* regret last night."

His eyes darkened and she could've sworn he was remembering all the things they'd done to, and with, each other in that hotel bed. Her throat was dry and she licked her lips. His gaze lowered to her mouth.

"Shouldn't the train be here any minute now?" She peered down the empty track, willing it to arrive. The sooner they got to the hotel, the sooner she might be able to talk him into a little nap, if that smoldering look on his face was any indication of how he was feeling.

With a roar that echoed the turmoil inside her, the train finally appeared and screeched to a stop, doors swishing open. It was going to be a long two hours back to the hotel.

Barely glancing at her, Clay ushered her ahead of him and into one of the train cars. She found a seat, plopping down across from an elderly man. She smiled at him, and he smiled wistfully back.

When she reached that gentleman's age, she hoped she'd done most of the things she'd wanted to do. No more hiding from the world, regretting what she hadn't tried. She was so glad she hadn't let that threat stop her from coming here.

The train gasped as the doors shut and it jerked to a start. Wait. Clay hadn't taken his seat.

She twisted in her chair to search behind her and spied him talking to the conductor. He was exchanging cash for tickets. Had she neglected to buy round-trip this morning? He glanced over his shoulder and caught her watching him and—oh my, the look in his eyes. She felt his desire all the way from the end of the train car.

After nodding to the conductor, he strode down the aisle toward her and offered his hand. "Come on."

Gabby jumped up, grabbed her purse and the packages she'd bought at the souvenir shop, and took his hand. "Where are we going?"

A muscle in his jaw ticked and then his brows rose. "Did you know that these international trains have sleeper cars?" His hand closed tightly around hers as he led her away.

Relishing the feel of her hand in his strong, callused one, she followed him willingly, happily, through two train cars until he stopped before a private compartment and ushered her inside.

She already had one boot unzipped and tugged off as he stepped in and locked the door behind him. Even as he shrugged out of his jacket, he cupped her face in his palm and kissed her, deep and hungrily.

Her mouth devoured his, desperate for his heat, his taste. Last night hadn't been nearly enough. Maybe she would never get enough of him. Her hands trembled as she tried to unbutton his flannel shirt and she moaned in frustration. She might've even popped a couple of his buttons in her hurry to get his clothes off.

He didn't even bother with her buttons. He untucked her blouse, lifted it over her head and reached behind her to unhook her bra. He kissed her madly as he shucked his jeans and only managed to get one leg of her slacks and panties off before she fell backward onto the small bunk.

Emitting a low sound from the back of his throat, he dropped to his knees, put his hands at her hips and pressed kisses to her stomach. Part of her watched as if from a distance, incredulous that this stunning man wanted her, *nerdy Gabby*, as much as she wanted him. How could that even be possible? But why question her luck?

Cradling his head in her hands, she lifted a foot to the edge of the mattress as he spread her thighs.

His mouth consumed her, played with her. His

tongue licked and teased. She gave a brief thought to how soundproof the sleeper car might or might not be, but didn't care. She moaned and whimpered, encouraging him, digging her heels into the mattress.

Opening her eyes, she couldn't help but stare as he used his mouth and fingers to pleasure her. The sight of him loving her overwhelmed her emotions and took her over the edge. She stiffened and cried out his name. She was still in the throes of incredible pleasure when he rolled on protection, then rose up over her and slid inside her.

He settled his elbows on either side of her head and kissed her jaw and behind her ear. His breathing was labored and she felt puffs of warm air on her shoulder as he moved his hips in a strong rhythm designed to build tension in her again.

Quickly, she locked her ankles around his narrow waist, ran her hands over his shoulders and clung to him, savoring the way he felt inside her, cherishing these moments with him. They still had tonight, after the dinner. And if she was really lucky, maybe even after the conference was over they could meet at his place on the weekends for a while...

Clay gave a final thrust that pressed deep and he stilled, straining until he relaxed against her, leaving kisses on her cheek and under her jaw.

She wasn't sure how long they lay there together, sideways on the tiny bunk, nuzzling and dozing. But the train ride, she reminded herself, would take two hours. She grinned and tightened her arms around him. That should give them plenty of opportunity for a second round.

HE'D REALLY SCREWED up this time.

Clay opened drowsy eyes and watched the mountainous countryside pass by outside the train window. His head was pillowed on Gabby's soft breast and he nuzzled it even as he knew he should get up and get dressed.

He and Gabby had ended up snuggled together on one of the single bunks. She still had one pant leg shoved around her ankles. What was wrong with him? He'd never had to have a woman so desperately that he couldn't wait until she had all her clothes off. Never had sex felt so wild, or had he fallen into such a lethargic sleep afterward.

Hadn't he decided this morning that making lo— having sex—with Gabby last night had been a mistake? He'd woken up in the middle of the night and watched her as she mumbled and burrowed even closer to him. Before he realized what he was doing, he'd picked up a strand of her long hair and wound it around his finger. He'd thought how soft it was and even brought it to his nose to inhale her unique fragrance.

As soon as he'd realized what a sap he was being, he'd moved back to the couch. No way he could've stayed there snuggling with her the rest of the night. He wasn't that kind of guy. Why'd he have to keep reminding himself of this?

But she got under his skin like nobody else. From the minute she'd disappeared this morning, through the fight that ended as abruptly as it had begun and her contagious enthusiasm for that particle accelerator machine, she rattled him. She threw him off balance.

She moaned and stirred beneath him, so he tried to rise, but she held on. "You don't have to get up."

They still had an hour or so before they arrived in Lucerne. So, no, he guessed he didn't have to leave her arms just yet.

CLAY TUGGED AT his bow tie. This rented penguin suit restricted his movement. He checked his shoulder holster again for the Sig Sauer, feeling vulnerable without the backup piece he usually kept in his boot. Another reason why he hated penguin suits. The pinching, shiny dress shoes.

"Okay, I'm ready."

At the sound of fabric swishing, Clay spun. "About ti—" Someone hit the pause button on his brain.

"Clay?"

He closed his mouth and swallowed, his throat suddenly dry. Was this extraordinary beauty really Gabby? She wore makeup that made her eyes look smoky and sultry. Her long hair was pulled up in a smooth twist with a couple of curling tendrils framing her face. The style looked both elegant and sexy. He wanted to press his lips to the vulnerable spot at the nape of her neck.

Sparkly earrings dangled from her ears, but her throat was bare. Until this moment he'd never in his life had the urge to buy a woman jewelry.

Her deep blue gown sparkled like she was wearing the night sky with twinkling stars. It plunged in a V between her breasts, showing just a hint of soft, plump cleavage. The lower part fit close to her curvy hips and then pooled on the floor.

He knew that body now. Knew the suppleness of her skin, the fragrance of her excitement, the sounds she made in the throes of passion. He pictured her the way she'd been in his arms this afternoon, his mouth on that golden skin, all the things he'd done to her. All the things she'd done to him. He closed his eyes, remembering.

"Clay?"

He opened them as she smoothed her hands down those curvy hips. "Do I look all right?"

All right? She was the most sensuously beautiful woman he'd ever known. And the connection between them was undeniable. His body still shuddered from the intensity of their short time in that narrow train bunk.

As they were getting dressed in the sleeper car she'd beamed with happiness and hope. Hope for something he could never give her. Despite her assurances, her feelings were all wrapped up in some unrealistic fantasy... Whatever Gabby wanted in a guy, it wasn't him.

He needed to make sure she realized that when they touched down in New York tomorrow, he'd be walking away without a backward glance. At least, that was the plan.

But her in that dress right now? Definitely a major obstacle to the plan.

"Is something wrong?" She spun and then peeked over her shoulder at him, running her hands over the tight-fitting backside of the dress. "My gown? Is it inappropriate?"

"What?" He cleared his throat trying to find his voice. "No. It's fine." He had to drag his gaze away from her to look at his watch. "We better get going."

With a slight quirk of her lips she accompanied him

down to the hotel ballroom, where he fetched her a glass of champagne, and played the doting boyfriend. In the back of his mind he worried that the role came way too easily to him.

After the chairman of some Swiss bank wrapped up his speech, dinner was served. Clay swallowed his goblet of water in one long gulp, and then dug into his salad. Every few minutes, he scanned the perimeter of the room. But as the salads were cleared away a twinge of pain stabbed behind his eyes and at his temples.

As the waiter set the dinner plate in front of him, his head was pounding and his vision had blurred. Was he getting the flu? As he picked up his fork his hand shook. Something was wrong. Without excusing himself to Gabby, he jumped up from the table and bolted for the men's room.

He barely made it to a stall in time before he lost the water and salad. He was sweating, clammy, cold. So cold. Shivering, he didn't have the strength to get up. His last thought before the world went black was for Gabby. Someone had taken him out. And now she was unprotected.

"FAMILY FOR CLAYTON BELLAMY?"

Gabby jerked up from the hospital waiting room chair and waved at the doctor. "Yes, that's me. How is Clay? Is he going to be all right?"

"You are his wife?" The doctor peered at Gabby over her glasses.

Though Gabby didn't know how to contact Clay's family, she'd left a message at the base in Virginia

Beach. But she wasn't going to wait for someone else to make decisions if he needed surgery now. She might get in trouble later, but… "Yes."

"He is stable now. But the blood pressure and body temperature had dropped very low, so we want to keep him overnight for to watch." The doctor's thick German accent made it difficult to understand her, but Gabby caught her meaning. "We are flushing his system with IV. You say he is not allergic to anything?"

"No. I said I didn't know." Gabby bit her lip. Trying to answer the paramedic's questions earlier had been like a smack in the face. Blood type? She didn't know. Medical history? No idea. She'd only met him a couple of months ago. And in that time she'd only spent a total of nine days with him.

And yet, she knew him. His quiet confidence. His humble strength. The fact that he would give his life for his country. Or even just to help someone in need… She almost broke down.

Drawing a steadying breath, she met the doctor's questioning gaze. "Have you figured out what's wrong with him?"

The doctor looked at the chart in her hands. "Well, we want to run couple more tests, but maybe some kind of toxin was introduced into his system."

"Toxin?" Her vision blurred as tears filled her eyes. "You mean, like, a poison?" Oh, Clay. Oh, Clay.

"I cannot say. But I have notified the *polizei*," the doctor continued. "They will wish to speak at you."

Gabby clamped a hand over her mouth. This was her fault.

The doctor gripped her upper arm. "He will be all right. You have someone to be with you?"

Gabby nodded, glancing back at James. He was sitting in a row of chairs, legs crossed at the knee, watching her. He smiled, returning her nod.

He'd shown up not long after she'd raced to follow Clay. When she'd hesitated to invade the men's restroom, James had gone in. He'd been the one to call emergency services. And he'd been so supportive, so kind. He seemed genuinely worried about Clay.

"Can I see him?" she asked the doctor now.

The doctor hesitated. "Ya, once we move him to room, okay?"

Wiping the tears off her cheeks, Gabby nodded again, and then returned to sit next to James and fill him in.

James took her hand in his. "I'm concerned about you, Gabby. You need to rest. I could stay. Why don't you go back to the hotel for a while?"

Gabby pulled her hand from his, clasped both of hers in her lap. "Thank you for offering, but I couldn't."

"It's only a few blocks away," James persisted. "You could be back here within minutes once he wakes up."

"I'm not leaving him! You go if you want. I'll be fine."

James's brow furrowed. "Of course not. I just wanted to be helpful." He slumped in his chair, staring at the floor. "I feel so useless."

"I'm sorry to snap." She put her hand on his shoulder. "It means a lot to me that you're here."

He raised his head, his eyes soft, adoring. "Does it? Because that's all that's important to me. To mean something to you. To be there for you when you need me." He took her hand again. "I want us to…" He leaned closer, cupped her cheek in his palm.

Gabby stiffened. "James…"

"I can be everything to you, Gabby." There was a desperate quality to his voice. "You don't need that guy." He jerked his head in the general direction of the outer waiting room door. "You need me."

"No." Wrenching away, she jumped to her feet.

"I'm sorry. I'm sorry." He sounded panicked, not sorry.

"Mrs. Bellamy?"

"James, I…appreciate you being here, but…"

"Mrs. Clayton Bellamy?"

Oh, that was *her*. "But I think you should go." Gabby spun to face the nurse. But not before she caught a glimpse of something cross James's face. She got that he was disappointed, frustrated even. But he'd seemed…furious. She walked off without looking back. "Yes, that's me."

At the nurse's directions, Gabby took the elevator and found Clay's room. She pushed through the door and had to compose herself before approaching the bed. Seeing Clay so pale, so unmoving… What had she done to him?

She took his hand and caressed it, noting all the scars and calluses, how it dwarfed hers. She studied his face, relaxed in sleep, the strong nose, the thick lower lip. Already his cheeks sported a five o'clock shadow.

Glancing around, she pulled the straight-backed chair up close and took his hand again, willing him to get better.

How could she live with herself if he didn't?

15

CLAY BLINKED AWAKE. His blurry gaze followed a long, dark strand of hair curled against the white sheet covering his stomach. It had slipped from Gabby's fancy hairdo. She was sitting in a chair next to his bed, but she'd fallen asleep with her head lying on the mattress. Her hair was mussed, her makeup smudged and she was holding his hand. His chest tightened. Damn, she was beautiful.

He blinked again and the fuzziness dissipated. He scanned white walls, a rolling bedside tray, the IV in his arm. He was in a hospital. The banquet. He remembered drinking water, eating salad and then... He swallowed. Had he been drugged? Had Gabby?

She seemed uninjured, but, how long had he been out? What had happened while he was incapacitated? He curled his fingers more tightly around hers. "Gabby?"

Her eyes opened and she looked at him. That slow smile and the warmth in her gaze... He had a crazy thought that he wanted to wake up to that every morning.

Then her smile was replaced with a stricken expression and she shot up in the chair. "Clay!"

"Hey." His throat was dry, his body a bit weak. But he gave her a reassuring smile.

She stood. "I'm going to get the doctor."

"Wait." He kept hold of her hand. "Are you okay?" His voice was raspy. "No one hurt you or threatened you?"

"Me?" Her eyes widened. "*I'm* fine. You were the one who was poisoned."

Poisoned? Someone had gotten close enough to put something in his food or drink. Some bodyguard he'd turned out to be. Had it been meant for Gabby? His stomach clenched just thinking what could have happened to her.

What if it hadn't been a mistake? What if someone had intentionally tried to take him out, leaving Gabby vulnerable? This threat might be bigger than he'd originally thought. He needed to call Neil. He threw back the sheet and tried to swing his legs off the bed.

"Clay!" Rushing in, Gabby planted her hands on his chest and pushed him back. "What do you think you're doing?"

"I need my phone," he mumbled, but he was weaker than he thought and slumped back against the pillow.

"Stay in bed." She pushed the call button. "A nurse should be in to check on you in a minute."

"Gabby, listen to me."

One of her hands was still flattened on his chest and he covered it with his. "If they got to me that easily, you need more security."

"I already talked to the police. They're questioning everyone. But Clay, I'm so sorry." He looked up to find her eyes filled with tears. "This is all my fault."

He scoffed.

"It's true." She looked down at their hands. "You'd be safe in Virginia Beach right now if it wasn't for me."

He shook his head. "You mean, maybe I'd be safe in some war zone? *That* kind of safe?"

She smiled ruefully and her eyes twinkled like the sparkles in her dress. "Okay. Point taken."

His chest eased at her smile.

"But you know what I mean." She bit her lip in that adorable way. "Protecting me isn't the same as protecting the country."

"Maybe it is." Some crazy impulse made him bring her hand to his lips.

Gabby searched his face, a question in her eyes. But he didn't have any answers. He tugged her down to sit beside him, wrapped his arms around her and held her tight. All he knew was he had her where he wanted her. Where he needed her right now. The soft, warm weight of her against his chest eased the bleakness.

She rubbed her cheek on his collarbone, her hands caressing his arms, then shoulders. He arched into her touch like a cat being petted. Lowering his nose to her hair, he closed his eyes and inhaled. "What's your perfume?"

She lifted her chin and settled her lips just under his jaw. "Gardenias. You like it?"

"Yes," he said with a surrendering sigh. He stared at her a moment, then framed her face in his palms and kissed each corner of her mouth, her nose, her eyes.

Desperate to taste her, he fit his mouth to hers. She responded instantly, moaning, deepening the kiss. He loved that about her, how she could give all of herself to a kiss. If only he could absorb all her tender goodness, all her generous compassion, all her confident love, then maybe they'd have a chance...

Wait. Have a chance with Gabby? They must have given him some kind of pain meds. A chance at what? Years of making each other miserable? What had he been thinking? He'd forgotten his mission for a minute there. Keep Gabby safe. He didn't understand what was going on, but he hadn't come this far and spent this amount of time just to be careless now.

So best place to keep Gabby safe? Back on home turf. He felt like a sitting duck in this hospital. He checked the clock on the opposite wall. Their train for Zurich had already left, but taking a different flight, or even a different route, was safer, anyway. He needed his phone. And his clothes. He eased Gabby away from him. "We have to get out of here. Can you get my stuff?"

"Clay," she said his name like a gentle scolding and smoothed her fingers through the hair at his temple. "Right now the most important thing is to make sure the poison is out of your system."

"I'm fine."

She gaped at him. "You can't be. Not this soon."

He stared at her. "Okay. Why don't you get the nurse? And bring me some water. I'm really thirsty."

She jumped up. "Of course. I'll be right back."

As soon as she cleared the threshold to the hallway, he sat up and swung his legs over the edge of the bed.

Grimacing, he ripped off the tape holding his IV and then yanked the needle out of the crook of his arm.

For a minute, the room spun. He used his hospital gown to stop the bleeding from the IV while he rummaged through the only cabinet and found his stuff.

But he'd barely gotten a quick text shot off to Neil before Gabby reappeared with a glass of water.

"What are you doing?" She set the cup down and rushed to him. "Get back in bed. The nurse is coming."

Clay ignored her and searched online to make new travel arrangements, though he did drink the water and thank her for it. He could email the hotel once they were on the train. Have the concierge pack and ship their belongings to the airport. They weren't going back to the Palace Lucern.

"Clay, please." She put her hand on his arm and when he looked up, it was to pleading dark eyes.

Shaking off her hand, he set down his phone and grabbed his clothes from the cabinet. The penguin suit would have to do.

"Will you at least—" Gabby started.

"No. This is nonnegotiable. Get your coat. We're leaving now."

He held her stare while she studied him. She must've decided he wasn't going to change his mind, because she slowly stepped over to the chair and gathered up her wrap and purse. As he dressed—slowly and with Gabby's help—the nurse came in, but once Clay agreed to sign a "discharged against doctor's orders" form, they caught the first cab to the train station.

Twelve hours later they were landing at Kennedy

Airport, though in local time it was still the same day they'd left. Clay had slept for most of the flight, or dozed as best he could. What he needed to tell Gabby had to be done when he could say his piece and then walk away.

Once they were through customs, the new bodyguard was waiting for them with a sign.

Gabby halted a few steps behind him. She'd been unusually quiet most of the trip, occasionally stealing glances at him with wary eyes. "We didn't discuss this."

Clay turned back. "Gabby, I have to be in Little Creek."

"I know that." Her lips compressed and she folded her arms under her breasts.

When she said nothing more, he took her silence as acceptance and confirmed the guy's credentials before handing Gabby's carry-on to him and asking him to meet her at the luggage carousel. Then he faced Gabby, a lump in his throat.

If he'd thought at all about how this thing with her would end, he'd hoped after they caught her stalker, she would return to her world, and he'd go back to Little Creek and maybe they'd exchange a few polite texts until his next mission took him out of the country...

"I asked Neil to have someone look into the wait staff at the Palace Lucern, but I believe it's more likely a colleague of yours. We're focusing on the five of them who were there."

She nodded. "I agree. Though I hate to think one of them would be capable of this, it does narrow it down. But the investigation in Switzerland sounds expensive. I can't really afford—"

"Don't worry about it."

She raised disapproving brows. "I didn't argue when you insisted on leaving the hospital, but I draw the line at you metaphorically patting my pretty little head. Ultimately, I need to make my own decisions regarding my safety."

She frowned and bit her lip. "I'm aware that I dragged you into this mess by showing up at your base and falling apart. But that doesn't mean I need twenty-four-hour protection. I feel safer now with the security you had installed in my apartment and I *will* repay you for that. But I won't let you pay for anything else, and I can't afford a bodyguard."

"Until we can—"

"Can we just…sit for a minute?" Gabby gestured at a nearby coffee shop. "Talk?"

He hesitated, glancing between the café and the baggage claim exit. "All right." Resigned, he followed her to a table. He couldn't decide if he was hoping she would end things, or desperately hoping she wouldn't.

No, of course he was hoping she would.

She settled into her chair and met his gaze with steady coffee-colored eyes. "I had a lot of time to think when I was down in that well in Paraguay. And I promised myself that if I got out of there alive I'd stop being such a coward in my personal life, so I'm just going to say this." She wrung her hands, but then lifted her chin. "I—I have feelings for you, Clay."

His heart thumped a little faster. The hardest thing he ever did was look away, lean back in his chair. "You only think you do. It's Savior Syndrome. It's a thing. But the feelings aren't real." Just like his feelings wouldn't last either. It was the nature of the beast.

She folded her arms. He could feel her stare weighing on him, but if he looked into her eyes, he might lose his resolve.

"One way to prove you wrong is to give us a chance," she said quietly. "Time will tell."

She was such an optimist. "Time would prove me right. Look, SEALs deploy on a moment's notice with no idea when they'll return or even *if* they'll return. It wouldn't be fair to you—"

Her lips flattened. "That sounds like an excuse." She dropped her gaze to her hands, where she was shredding a tissue. "If you don't care for me, then why would you use your leave and fly to Switzerland just to watch out for me?"

He licked his dry lips. Okay, so he cared about her. Right now. Cared too much to let her think anything would come of it. She was way too good, too smart, too everything for him, anyway. So, he'd have to be brutal. He looked her straight in the eye. "Look, Gabby. You want a fun night in the sack?" He shrugged. "I'm your guy. But I will never want all the complications that come with being in a relationship. I know what you want, Gabby, and I'm not it." He caught her flinch from the corner of his eye and gritted his teeth.

Her lips rolled in as she slowly nodded. "Right." She grabbed her purse and got to her feet. "Well, at least I didn't wimp out this time." She gave him a tight smile. "I feel like I've said this before but have a nice life."

"Gabby." He jumped to his feet and reached for her

arm. But what did he even want from her? He wanted her to leave. And he wanted her to never leave.

"What?" Her head tilted, her eyes questioning, hoping.

No sense in giving her false hope. He dropped his hand. "Nothing."

She blinked rapidly as her eyes filled with tears. Those tears were killing him.

Preparing to let her go, he watched as she headed toward the café door. Then she turned back to him. "Maybe you're wrong, you know?" she breathed the words softly.

But he knew he wasn't. He huffed a bitter laugh. "You don't know me, Gabby. That's what I've been trying to tell you. You have this fantasy in your head of who I am." The thought of losing hero status in her eyes made his throat ache.

She drew herself up, hardened her expression. "Are you sure you know yourself as well as you think?" Then she spun on her boot heels and bolted from the café.

The urge to run after her and catch her in his arms almost brought him to his knees. He knew he was doing the right thing. But why did the right thing have to twist him up inside?

16

GABBY SQUEEZED BETWEEN two other subway commuters and got a tenuous hold on a metal pole when the doors closed. As she took in the packed car, she smiled at the thought of the huge guy Clay had hired to be her bodyguard trying to fit onto this train.

Yesterday morning, while waiting for her luggage, she'd told the nice bodyguard guy that Clay had changed his mind and would be staying with her, so he wouldn't be needed. That way, he wouldn't report back to his boss that she was unprotected. Mostly because she couldn't afford him. But she also hadn't received any more threats. And between the apartment's new security system, the pepper spray she kept with her at all times and the self-defense classes, she felt as safe as any regular person would.

And she'd be sure to spread it around the office that she and Clay had broken up. That way he wouldn't be in any danger.

She exited the subway to face another chilly, gray

day, so she opened her umbrella. It was as if the weather knew that a warm, sunny April would be wasted on her, knew that bright spring flowers blooming would only depress her more. New York clung to winter as desperately as Gabby clung to her numbness. If she didn't let herself think about Clay, then maybe she could regain a sense of normalcy.

Trying to do just that, she spent the morning whittling down the stack of reports that had built up while she was in Switzerland. Coworkers talked over partitions, describing their weekends, a couple asking her about Switzerland, and she talked about the Hadron Collider and the beautiful hotel.

She *would* get over this. She *would* get on with her life. And she certainly didn't have this…Savior Syndrome.

Curled up in bed yesterday, she'd researched Savior Syndrome online and read all the articles she could find. Disturbing phrases like "unhealthy relationships" and "victim mentality" had popped out at her. One of the articles said that some women find being rescued "romantic" and will seek out men who are controlling or emotionally unstable. Had she done that?

Everything inside her vehemently denied that accusation. Clay hadn't tried to control her. Well, maybe a little. Like installing a security system in her apartment without asking her. And trying to tell her she couldn't go see the Hadron Collider. At least he'd relented on that. But then he'd hired a bodyguard without consulting her. Omg, he *was* controlling.

And he was, at the very least, that most horribly clichéd of terms: emotionally unavailable.

It'd seemed as if there were two Clays. The first one, who'd kissed her with so much tenderness, had made her want to see where the relationship might go. And the other Clay, a player who didn't do relationships because they were messy.

But when she thought about it now, she could also see the hurt little boy inside whose parents had made him believe they didn't care. The boy who'd learned not to believe in happy marriages. How sick was it that she still wanted, desperately, to be the one to make him believe in love?

She'd thought she was falling in love with Clay, and even started to believe that he had feelings for her, too. But how could she trust her judgment? Maybe she'd just been trying to have her own fairy-tale romance. A soldier had saved her life, and she'd wanted that sappy happy-ever-after.

"So, you got home okay?"

Startled, Gabby spun in her chair to face James. "What? Oh yeah, we just took a later flight." She tried to smile.

He stuck his hands in his pockets and leaned against her desk. His stare weirded her out. She hadn't seen him since he'd acted so creepy at the hospital, and she had to admit she'd arrived extra early this morning to avoid him. "I broke up with Clay," she blurted.

He perked up. "Really?"

She tried not to roll her eyes. That had not been a hint. "Want to get some lunch?"

Uh... No. Not if she was starving and he held the last bag of French fries on earth.

But she had to work with the guy. "Uh, it's raining, so..." She tilted her head and wrinkled her nose in a what-can-you-do expression.

"We could go to the deli across the plaza." He smiled. "My treat."

"Oh, uh..." Geez, this was so awkward. "I better not. I've got so much work to catch up on."

"Yeah, yeah," He nodded. "Okay. What about dinner tonight?"

Gabby blinked. So was he asking her out on a date again? Hadn't they already been there, done that? The guy did not know how to take no for an answer. And she couldn't keep making excuses. Or coming in early to avoid him. She sighed. Maybe it was time to be more...forceful. Tell him in no uncertain terms that it wasn't happening.

Shoulders squared, she scooted back her chair and drew in a deep breath. "James, I appreciate that you've been a good friend to me. But I'm totally not interested in being anything more than coworkers, so I need you to stop asking me out."

His smile vanished, his face turned red and his lips twisted into a snarl. He reeled and stalked off.

Well, that could've gone better.

She looked around and noticed everyone in the immediate area had their heads poked above or around the corners of their cubicles.

Oh no. Maybe she should've taken him somewhere

more private to do that. She squeezed her eyes closed. *Way to humiliate the guy, Gabby.*

She'd better go apologize. Otherwise it would worry her the rest of the day. Get it over with before he retaliated.

Now why did she think he might react vindictively?

Dreading the encounter, she stood and made her way over to James's cubicle, rehearsing an appropriate apology in her mind.

But he wasn't there.

Relief swamped her. She'd leave him a note. That would be better anyway, to be able to word it just so.

But his desk was completely clear except for his laptop. Not a pen or pencil, not one piece of notepaper or post pad to be had. Wow.

She yanked open the top drawer and grabbed a worn spiral notebook. A chain was caught on the metal rings as she lifted the notebook from the drawer. It was some sort of necklace, a silver—medal. *Her* Mary medal!

She'd never understood the phrase "make my skin crawl" until now.

"What are you doing?"

She jumped, floundering a moment, and almost dropped the necklace as she swung around to face him. "James."

"You were snooping in my things?"

Seriously? He was accusing her of wrongdoing? She almost choked on her anger. "This is *my* medal." She held it up as evidence. "Why do *you* have it? I thought I'd lost it during the mugging."

The guy in the next cubicle stuck his head over the partition.

James swallowed, shifted weight from one foot to the other and finger-combed his hair off to the side with the opposite hand. "I found it. And I meant to return it, and then I kept forgetting and leaving it at my apartment." He flashed a smile. "Until today."

Gabby clasped the medal tightly in her hand. He was so obviously lying. If that was true why hadn't he given it to her a moment ago when he came by her cubicle?

But what could she accuse him of? Stealing her medal? She had no proof. Maybe he had gone back like she had, except he'd spotted the keepsake. If that was true, then the worst he had done was neglect to return it. And even if he had planned on keeping it, she had it back now. The police wouldn't be able to do anything.

Trying to school her features, she managed a tight smile. "I am glad to have it again, at least." She brushed past him and practically ran to her desk to hug herself and pace.

She had to think this through. Had James really just found it after the mugging and forgotten to return it? If not, why would he want to keep her medal? Maybe as a token of him saving her? And come to think of it, he had chased away that mugger a little too easily that night...

An ice-cold chill shivered down her spine. James knew where she lived. Could he have made a copy of her dead bolt key and broken into her apartment? But why?

But the more she thought about it, the more the clues

came together. James had been at the conference and so conveniently nearby when Clay was poisoned. He'd even tried to make a play for her at the hospital.

All her suspicions coalesced into certainty. James had been so solicitous, so friendly. But it was all a lie. Why hadn't she seen that before? Was she that naive, doomed to misjudge all men?

Her stomach lurched. She was going to be sick.

She started to dash out of her cubicle but James blocked her path. She almost ran into him. "James!"

"Gabby?" He cupped her shoulders roughly and she had to stop herself from shaking him off.

She made herself smile. "Yes?" *Keep your expression neutral.*

He squeezed her shoulders and squinted at her. "Are you okay?"

It was on the tip of her tongue to demand answers, to ask him how, why he'd tormented her. But she wouldn't be the victim who stupidly confronted the villain instead of going to the authorities. Though she wasn't ready to go to the police yet. Not until she knew for sure.

She licked her lips. "I'm fine." *Keep smiling.*

"You don't look fine." His smile was wide but menacing, his body almost touching hers.

Make something up and get out! "Yeah, you know?" She frowned and nodded, even rubbed her stomach for good measure. "I may have picked up a bug on the plane. I'll take the rest of the day off." She clamped a hand over her mouth. "I think I'm going to be sick." And she wasn't lying.

James dropped his hands and stepped back, and she hurried down the hall to the ladies' room.

She slumped against a wall and started shaking and crying. Maybe she'd just spend the rest of the day in there.

At least until she could figure out what to do about her psycho coworker.

TWO DAYS AFTER arriving back at Little Creek, Clay shipped out to northern Iraq with the rest of his team and was preparing to assist Kurdish and Iraqi forces in a hostage retrieval operation. It felt good to get back to the mission. This was what his life was about. *This* he excelled at.

Eventually, Gabby would realize he'd done her a favor. He kept telling himself that every time he pictured her walking out of that airport coffee shop with that shattered look on her face. *"Maybe you don't know yourself."*

He closed his eyes. He did know. She did want more than he could give. More than he could be.

But why was he so bothered now? Hadn't he wanted her to lose the rose-colored glasses she saw him through? Mission accomplished, right? He'd done all he could do. Neil was investigating her five coworkers. She had a new bodyguard. He could move on.

"You rub that firearm any harder, Hounddog," L.T. called from across the bunker, "and I'll think maybe you two should get a room."

The rest of the guys hooted.

Clay gave them all the one-finger salute, then set

his cleaning rag aside and started reassembling his assault rifle.

But L.T. was right. Clay needed to get his head in the game. Tonight's mission was going to be tricky. His SEAL team was technically only there to "advise and assist." But, yeah, that was just on paper. A dozen hostages were due to be executed soon, and his team, along with a Delta Force team, were moving in tonight.

Clay geared up, listened as L.T. went over the plan with the group one last time and then headed out into the night.

Gunshots popped and bullets whizzed past him as they invaded the compound. What Intel had thought was a dozen hostages turned out to be more like five dozen. That unexpected contingency created chaos getting them all out, ushering them down winding, cramped hallways and assessing each hostage for bombs and weapons before helping them into overloaded Humvees.

Clay was laying down cover fire when a bright light flashed and he was blown yards away. He landed on his back with a hard thud and his chest felt like it was on fire. All he could hear was a loud ringing in his ears and all he could see was black smoke.

But his last thought was of Gabby.

17

THEY WERE CHASING HER. Her heart pounded in her chest. Thorns caught on her blouse and ripped a gash in her arm as she crashed through the thick foliage. Blood beaded through the bright white silk. She couldn't catch her breath and felt a sharp pain in her side, but she couldn't stop running. She had to get to Clay. He needed her.

Her feet caught on something in her path and she went down hard, catching her fall with her hands. Disoriented, she glanced around and saw what had tripped her. Clay's lifeless body lay beneath her.

Then she looked up at the shadow behind her. Poised over her with rage glowing in his murderous eyes... The shadow was James.

She screamed.

Gabby jerked awake.

Whoa. She swallowed and took a breath. She had an appointment with the counselor today, but after finding her medal in James's desk yesterday she didn't need a psychiatrist to interpret *that* dream.

How she wished she could throw the covers over her head and sleep the day away. But she had to start dealing with her problems. And that meant calling a locksmith for one, and getting to work this morning for another, despite having to face James.

Keep your enemies close, right? At least if he was at work, she could keep her eye on him.

But when she arrived at the office and casually inquired after him in the break room, Samantha, another junior analyst, told her he'd called in sick with the flu and might be out all week. Gabby's whole body relaxed. He wasn't here. She wouldn't have to deal with him today. Or maybe even the entire week. Her hand flew to her Mary medal. It was back around her neck where it belonged, so maybe things would get better.

Now that he realized she was on to him, he must've given up. He knew that if he caused any more problems she'd know who to blame. For the first time in days, she took a deep, cleansing breath. Maybe between her counselor appointment this afternoon and having her medal again, she could begin to move on from all that had happened.

She desperately needed to move on.

Feeling a twinge of hope, she took her coffee to her cubicle and pulled out her phone.

@nerdybankanalyst
#gettingbacktonormal And to that end, another #bankingpunoftheday Bankers never die...they just pass the buck

"WHEN CAN I get the all clear, Doc?" Clay waited impatiently on the paper-covered examining table.

The Navy doctor pulled reading glasses down off his head and consulted Clay's chart. "No internal injuries. Just the concussion, some cracked ribs. I see you were treated for second-degree burns on the torso. No fever?" He felt Clay's forehead.

"No, sir," Clay answered. "I'm feeling great." Good enough, anyway. He'd lost a day in Iraq, and two days since he'd arrived in Virginia. He was itching to get back to active duty.

"I'd say a week, maybe ten days for the ribs to heal."

"A week! Come on, Doc, I feel fine."

The doctor scowled. "The head trauma alone is enough for me to bench you for two weeks."

Two weeks' medical leave? He'd go crazy.

As he headed over to his apartment, he reminded himself that he'd been lucky to come out of it with only a couple of burns and a few cracked ribs. So why didn't he feel lucky?

After waking up at the hospital at Kirkuk Regional Air Base, Clay had no memory of the night of the raid. But the last time he'd woken up in a hospital bed, Gabby had been clutching his hand.

Maybe it'd just been the long night on pain meds, but he'd wanted to see her one more time. And fix things with her. He just needed closure. Didn't like leaving things on such a bad note was all.

His sister had tried to contact him, but there'd been no calls or texts from Gabby. He'd texted Neil for an update on the Swiss investigation, but he put off listening to the numerous messages from his sister until he got stateside.

He and Ashley had never been close. He'd always wondered why, when they might have bonded over a common enemy, their stepfather. But from the beginning, the old man had treated Ashley differently. Not spoiled, by any means; she'd seen her fair share of discipline. But never the violent kind. That had been reserved for Clay.

Clay had been forced to conclude there was just something about him the old man had hated. Maybe his stepfather had seen Clay as a rival for his mother's affections. But that would've meant that his mother had to be affectionate with him. And she'd never been that. He'd never mattered to her.

Still sore—and okay, maybe he should've rested more today—he lay on the couch with the TV remote and woke up sometime in the middle of the night. He grabbed his phone. Three thirty-seven. Could he take another week of this?

He sat up gingerly and headed for the fridge, then remembered he didn't have any beer in the place. Barney's was closed. Heck, he wasn't supposed to drink with these pain meds, anyway.

But he needed…something. He was restless. He paced. Everything that had happened in recent months detonated in his mind, leaving fragments of depression, rage and misery bouncing around, still volatile.

Gabby trudging through the sweltering jungle with a smile. Or how she'd looked flushed with passion after he'd kissed her—right about where he was standing now. How she made him feel as if he...mattered.

That was a wild thought. He was a SEAL. What he did mattered. For a few more years, anyway. But Gabby...

Was she okay? What was she doing right now?

Sleeping, you moron.

Like a junkie needing a fix, he checked her Twitter page. Saw her most recent bank pun and smiled. Noticed the hashtag. Getting back to normal? He rubbed his chest at the sudden pang. That was good. Good for her. Getting back to normal. So, she hadn't received any more threats, or felt unsafe or had any further problems? She was getting on with her life.

That was a positive thing, right?

He shot off a text to Neil.

How are wedding plans coming?

Clay cringed and wiped a hand over his mouth. Wedding plans? He was truly desperate. He needed a hobby. His phone beeped.

You realize most people are asleep this time of night? What's up?

Clay grinned. Good old Barrow. He texted:

Bored. Another week medical leave. Let's go fishing.

Barrow: Bored? Yeah, right. Can't get away right now.
Why don't you go see a Broadway show?

Why would Neil think Clay cared about seeing a
Broadwa— Ah, Manhattan. Where Gabby lived. The
guy was still trying to play Cupid. Not cool, Barrow.
Clay hesitated, his thumb hovering over his phone. He
wasn't going to ask Neil about Gabby. He'd told himself
he could check in occasionally with her bodyguard. Tomorrow would be a week since he'd left her at Kennedy...

Nah, not into Broadway. Pool at Barney's more my
style. Just need my wingman.

Barrow: Maybe when this is all over.
Until then you should Charlie Mike.

Continue the mission? What was Barrow talking
about? What mission? His buddy was losing it, man.

Falling in LUV has fried your brain.
What mission?

Barrow: LUV is all that really matters, bro.
And Love IS the mission. Say hi to Gabby for me.

Clay flopped back on the couch and winced at the
pain in his ribs. Love was the mission? Say hi to Gabby?
He typed with his thumb, What are you talking about?
How would I tell Gabby anything?

Barrow: What? Aren't you with her? She told her bodyguard you were staying, so I assumed...

Clay jackknifed off the couch. She'd done what?
She didn't have anyone watching over her? And Neil
thought Clay was with her? Barrow didn't know he'd
been injured in Iraq. Clay stared at the phone, paralyzed.

But her Tweet had sounded like she was fine.

Of course, that Tweet had been four days ago...
Anything could've happened to her since then.

He would just call her and make sure. He brought
up her contact and—wait. It was four in the morning.
She'd be asleep.

Too bad. She shouldn't have fired the bodyguard if
she didn't want to get woken up.

On the other hand, if he called right now and she was
okay, he'd sound like a jerk. A lovesick jerk.

But he'd rather sound like a lovesick jerk than lay
here all night and worry about her.

His phone beeped.

Bellamy, you ARE in New York with Gabby, right?

Clay winced as he got to his feet, grabbed his duffel
and started throwing in some clothes. He would be as
soon as he could catch a flight out of here.

If he looked like a jerk, then so be it.

18

GABBY LOVED EASTER SUNDAY.

It might still be raining, but she headed out to Mass in her nicest dress, determined to move on with her life. To Charlie Mike.

Her throat tightened and her chest ached. She should get phrases like that out of her vernacular. They reminded her of Clay. And thinking of him... Her eyes watered. *Okay, stop it. Remember the long phone call you had with your family this morning.*

There, that helped.

In church, she said a prayer for James, hoping he was recovering from the flu, and that maybe they could at least work together without things being uncomfortable. And after Mass she stopped by the grocer's across from her place and splurged on a small ham, and ooh, fresh asparagus, and, yes, that potato salad looked good. She ended up buying way more than she should try to carry in only two bags, but she was right across the street.

When she set one bag down to use her key on the outer door, another resident of the building had come up behind her and used their key, so she walked in behind him. That must be how James had— No, she wouldn't think of that today.

"Hi, Gerard." She smiled at the elevator operator, but he didn't get up from his chair in the minuscule foyer. She should show Gerard James's picture, see if he recog—

"Power's out this side of the street." Gerard shook his head, grimacing at her full grocery bags. "You got to take the stairs, hon."

Ugh. Why had she bought so much food?

She trudged up four flights. Her arms were on fire as she set both bags down to unlock her dead bolt and open the door. Guess she didn't need to rush in to turn off the alarm.

She lugged the groceries to the kitchen and was putting things away in her dark fridge. Then she heard the sound of her dead bolt clicking shut.

She froze. With both arms full of groceries, she hadn't locked the door behind her... Spinning around with her heart banging in her chest, she faced—James. She couldn't breathe. She couldn't scream. And even if she'd wanted to run, she was literally cornered in her small kitchen.

"Hello, sweetheart." His sickly smile brought bile to her throat.

Sweetheart? She dragged in a breath and thought she might hyperventilate. Her pulse raced and she gulped air into her lungs. Her purse with her phone and the pepper spray was on the counter beyond her reach. Past James.

"What are you doing here?" Her voice was so shaky she stopped and tried to calm herself. But this, this invasion felt even more terrifying than the kidnapping had. At least then, she hadn't been alone.

James stepped closer and Gabby couldn't even back away. The edge of the counter cut into her back. "Gabby. I'm here for you, of course. I've always been here for you." She flinched away as he ran the back of his hand down her cheek.

"You were here before, right? You were the one who broke in and—destroyed my stuff?"

His smile dropped and he scowled. "I was really mad after you didn't want to go out with me again. You wanted to just be friends? But we're so much more than friends, Gabby. After what we went through together? No one else can understand. I thought you knew that. You went out with me, even made me dinner here, so I know you love me. You want to tease me, is that it?" he whined.

"No, that's not it." In her mind she was calculating whether she could reach into the drawer with the knives and grab one before he stopped her. And even if she managed that, could she actually stab him? Maybe it would be enough to scare him away. Get him to leave.

He closed the distance between them and put his mouth on hers.

Gabby twisted her head and leaned as far back as she could, shoving at his chest. But he was half a foot taller than her, and wiry strong.

His lips smashed against her cheek, her neck. "I know you love me, Gabby, you just don't want to admit it, right? But I saved you from that mugger, remember? I saved you." He tried kissing her again and finally Gabby remembered her self-defense training and jerked her knee into his groin. She wasn't tall enough to do much damage, but he jumped away and that was enough to give her a moment. She had a split second to decide, purse or knife. She went for the drawer and the first knife she spotted.

But James grabbed her wrist with a howl and for what seemed like an eternity they fought over possession of the knife. But with his superior height and weight and upper body strength, it wasn't really a fair match. He wrested the knife away from her and she screamed as he brought it to her throat.

CLAY PAID THE cabdriver and jogged up the steps to Gabby's building. He'd had Neil text him the address and then had to explain the whole situation to his buddy while he waited to board at the Norfolk airport.

When he rang the buzzer outside, no one answered, but through the glass door Clay saw an elderly man in a blazer stand up from a chair in the foyer.

He called through the door, "Power's out. You got to call 'em on their phone, then they can come down and let you in."

Clay raised his brows, yanked out his phone and called Gabby. Her phone went to voice mail. A sick feeling hit his stomach.

He knocked on the door and the building super got up again. "Do you know if Gabriella Diaz is home?"

The building super nodded. "Sure is. Just came in a few minutes ago."

Maybe she was in the restroom… Still, in his gut, Clay knew something was wrong. And he'd already decided he'd prefer to look like a jerk than sit by if she was in danger. He held up his phone to the man. "She's not answering, could you maybe knock on her door for me and make sure she's okay?"

"Me? Listen, that's four flights up." He shook his head. "I can't do that."

"She's had some threats lately, and I'm worried about her."

The super looked confused. "That why she had all that security installed?" He scratched his head. "Let me see some ID."

Clay pulled out his driver's license, and for good measure, his military ID.

The gray-haired man squinted through the glass door, reading Clay's ID. "You Navy? I served in the Navy. Vietnam." He pushed open the door. "Come on in out the rain, sailor."

Before the super had finished his sentence, Clay was bounding up the stairs. He tried to remember Gabby's apartment number. 4D. He was shaking as he took the stairs three at a time. Second floor. Third.

Once he reached the fourth floor, her door was the first one he saw past the landing. He knocked, long and loud.

No answer.

He called her phone again. Heard it ringing through the door. He pounded again. "Gabby! It's Clay. Let me in!"

"Clay!" It was Gabby. She screamed, sounded terrified!

"Gabby!" He didn't have a firearm to shoot the lock off since he'd had no time to clear a piece through airport security.

Cursing with every foul word he knew, he flew back down the stairs. What if he didn't get to her in time?

If something happened to her, he couldn't...

There had to be a window— "Call 911!" he ordered the super as he ran outside, down to the corner and into the narrow alley between two apartment buildings. Fourth floor... He calculated the layout of the apartments in his mind, and tried to judge which window would be Gabby's.

Time was passing too fast! Even now he could be too late. He made an educated guess and bolted up the fire escape, climbing rickety metal stairs to the fourth-story window and peered in.

His blood turned to ice. Gabby stood in her tiny living room, trapped in James's arms. But what truly paralyzed Clay was the knife James held to her heart.

GABBY'S BACK WAS pressed to James's front. She'd been trying to talk him down ever since she'd made a grab for the knife. But Clay pounding on her door had sent him into full-blown panic.

"This is your fault! You came on to me and then you rejected me. I was like some sick game to you!"

Every few words he jabbed the point of the knife into her chest. "Why did you do that to me? Why can't you just love me?" His voice wavered between a whine and a growl.

The alley window to her left crashed inward in a shower of glass. James jumped and turned toward the crash, giving Gabby a couple of seconds. But that was all she needed.

Grabbing his wrist, she shoved his hand holding the knife as hard as she could against the bookshelf and in the same instant, stomped his foot with her boot heel and popped her hips back to knock him off balance exactly like Clay had taught her.

James screamed and fell backward, hopping on his sore foot as Clay burst through the kicked-in window. Gabby wanted to run to him, but she made a dash for her purse and grabbed her pepper spray.

By the time she got back to the living room, Clay and James were locked in a struggle over the knife. "Clay!" She ran closer, snapped the cap off the pepper spray and aimed right for James's eyes.

As James shrieked and hollered, Clay moved in and put him in some sort of wrestling hold. Then he glanced at her. "Get me something to restrain him with."

Gabby couldn't think, she just stood there in shock and disbelief. She started shaking.

"Gabby! Look at me." Clay had James down on the floor, a knee between his shoulder blades, holding his arms in a tight grip behind his back. "Gabby, you have a stocking or uh, an extension cord?" He was talking slowly, as if she was a child.

She nodded and went to her closet to dig out her extension cord.

"Good, bring it here, now slip it around his wrists."

Gabby did so, still feeling as if she was moving in a trance. She watched as Clay finished tying up a crying, whimpering James.

Someone pounded on her door. Gabby froze inside.

"That would be the police. Answer the door." When she did, chaos and questions ensued as a bunch of officers took over. Clay remained at her side and kept his arm around her shoulders as the police questioned her.

While James was handcuffed and led away, Clay mentioned the knife and the policeman bagged it as evidence and hinted that a charge of assault with a weapon would be more likely to result in a long prison sentence.

Clay must've handled everything else because whatever happened next was all a blur. Somehow the broken window got covered with plastic, and the glass was cleaned up. It seemed so much later now, though she wasn't sure of the time. She only remembered Clay helping her get into her pajamas. Her hands were shaking, and so Clay unbuttoned her dress, murmuring gently how brave she'd been, how proud he was of her.

But when he opened the bodice and saw the little nicks from the knife, he cursed and paced away. "I wish I'd killed that—"

When he returned, he'd brought some ointment and bandages, a bottle of water and a couple of pills. Then he got her into her bed.

But she couldn't stop shivering. "Aw, Gabby, darlin'." He shucked his clothes, crawled in beside her and wrapped his arms around her. She was so cold and he was so warm. His heat enveloped her and she started crying, sobbing into his chest.

"It's okay, darlin'. Cry all you want," he mumbled, deep and raspy. His large hard body held her close.

Clay. He really was here. In her apartment. In her bed. She drew in a ragged breath and let it out on a wobbly sigh. Then she snuggled closer, rubbing her nose into his neck, and drifted off to sleep.

When she woke up sometime deep in the night, she stirred and looked up into Clay's soft brown eyes. He'd left the lamp on beside the bed and didn't seem to have slept at all. He smiled and smoothed a strand of hair from her face. Whether he admitted it or not, she saw more than just friendly concern in his eyes.

Gabby returned his smile, trying to signal that she was okay now, that she wasn't going to dissolve into a mess of hysterical tears again. She could feel his body—naked except for his boxers—against her, his hands rubbing her back, and she wanted him. She needed to make love with him.

She moved up and kissed him, running her hands over his shoulders and back, down his chest, and farther, slipping her fingers under the waistband of his underwear. She took hold of him. He was already hard and he moaned as she stroked him.

He deepened the kiss and rolled her to her back as he moved his mouth over her neck and throat.

She broke the kiss only to sit up and strip, toss her top and bottoms to the floor before grabbing a condom from her nightstand. "Make love to me, Clay," she whispered when she returned to his kisses.

He palmed her breast, lightly tweaking the nipple. She arched into his hand, wanting his weight over her, wanting him inside her. But he took his time, trailing kisses down her body, slowly bringing her skin to a tingly ache.

When he entered her, it was slow and deliberate. He held her gaze and filled her an inch at a time until he was deep in her core, and then stilled while he kissed her long and sensuously.

Only when she whimpered and lifted her hips did he begin to move, leisurely at first, almost reverently, while he smoothed her hair away from her face and kissed her eyes, her nose, her temples, her chin. His thrusts increased, his breathing quickened. He took her hands, entwining their fingers as he suckled her nipples, twirling his tongue over their hard tips.

When he came, he let out a faltering breath, his muscles strained and he held her so tightly. Neither of them said a word, but she could feel the love in the act. This wasn't sex for sex's sake. This was making love, whether he admitted it or not.

The next time she woke up, the sun was streaming through her bedroom window. She could hear birds chirping, but she knew before she opened her eyes that the other side of the bed was empty.

She sat up and scanned her small apartment, listened for sounds from the kitchen or bathroom, but all was profoundly quiet.

Clay was gone.

19

CLAY LIMPED DOWN to the doughnut shop a few blocks from Gabby's apartment building and ordered two coffees and a whole box of breakfast sandwiches, muffins and éclairs. He couldn't remember the last time he'd eaten.

His ribs hurt like hell, and the cut on his thigh from the broken window maybe should've had a couple of stitches, but he'd just wrapped it up in some gauze nice and tight. The pain would keep him alert. Maybe bring him clarity. And right now, more than anything, he needed clarity.

Or maybe he needed a gym with a punching bag. That usually cleared his mind real quick.

His thoughts were all jumbled and he couldn't seem to form coherent sentences. Everything was all…too much. He'd seen some scary things, but he'd never been as terrified as when he saw that knife at Gabby's chest.

And even more terrifying, he'd almost broken down last night making love to Gabby. Terror, and rage, and—whatever else he'd been holding in below the surface for weeks now—had threatened to boil over. She didn't need that from him. She'd needed a protector. And he hadn't even been able to do that.

He paid for the order and headed back.

When he let himself in with her key, she was sitting on the sofa, his duffel in her lap. She was cradling his bloody jeans against her and she looked up at him with tears in her eyes.

"Oh, Clay, there's so much blood." She held out the jeans to him as if he didn't already know they were a mess.

He set the breakfast on the coffee table, gently took the pants from her, stuffed them back in the duffel and set it aside. "It looks worse than it is."

She started shaking her head, looking confused. "How did you know? How are you here? You shouldn't be away from your base."

He moved around the table to sit beside her. "Shh, it's fine."

"But what if they call you and— Isn't that, like, AWOL or something?"

He put his arm around her, hoping she missed his wince. "I'm on medical leave."

She finally looked at him. "Why?"

"It doesn't matter. The important thing is, it's over now. You got him, Gabby. Pretty impressive move there, getting out of that hold."

She beamed up at him. "You saw that, huh? *You* taught me that move, and it worked."

"But, Gabby." He scowled. "Once you got away you didn't run. I told you to run."

"And leave you to fight off that creep by yourself?"

"Gabby, I'm a US Navy SEAL. I may not be good for much else, but I can fight."

She cupped his face in her hands, caressing his temple, his jaw. He closed his eyes, wanting to lean into her touch. "I would never leave you to fight alone. What kind of person would I be if I didn't try to help you?"

Uh, pretty much any other person on the planet.

People didn't stick their necks out for him. His team had each other's backs. That's what grunts like him did. But in this case, *he* wasn't supposed to be the one protected. He blinked at that thought. Remembered his mother standing by while his stepfather backhanded him across the face. And instead of rushing to shield him, she looked at him as if she was so disappointed in him for making her husband mad.

He'd hated those looks worse than the beatings.

Gabby's hands ran down his shoulders to rub his arms, bringing him back to the present. She framed his face again. "And what do you mean you're not good for much else? How can you say that? Clay, you're an incredible person. Disciplined, selfless, brave."

Clay blinked and looked into Gabby's eyes. She really believed that. Not only did she believe he was incredible, she'd risked her own safety to defend him. His fellow SEALs did that, that's what SEAL brothers did. But Gabby didn't have to. And yet, she hadn't even hesitated. Even after the way he'd left things with her a week ago.

Why would she do that? Unless she really did have feelings for him?

A yearning welled up in him. A need buried so deeply he hadn't even known what it was. But now that he recognized it, he felt it like a gaping hole. A pit he'd been trying to cover ever since he could remember. He wanted...needed someone to care. Someone to pray for his safe return. Someone to believe in him. Someone to have his back, no matter what.

He looked at Gabby again and he *saw* her. Saw how her eyes shone with concern. For him.

Was it too late to have more? Had he ruined his chances?

Before he lost all control of his emotions he put his arms around her and pulled her to him, grimacing as his cracked ribs complained.

But she didn't hug him. Slowly, she pulled out of his arms, sat back and dropped her gaze to her hands clasped in her lap. "Why did you come here?"

Why was she asking? Did she want him to leave? "Neil told me you fired your bodyguard."

She met his gaze, a hint of rebelliousness in her eyes. "Why should that matter to you?"

"Because it's— I was right, wasn't I? You weren't safe."

"My safety isn't your responsibility." Her tone was flat, dead.

He felt it like a physical pain. Like an imbecile, he'd left it too late. Lost his chance with her. He eased back against the couch, holding his ribs. Maybe they could start again. He'd take friendship. For now. "We're friends, aren't we?" He slid a glance over to her. She had a strange look on her face.

"What are you thinking?" he asked.

"You're in pain. You cut yourself breaking in the window, but why are you on medical leave?"

He hesitated. This is what wrecked a lot of soldiers' marriages. Facing the possibility of a partner's death every time they deployed took a lot of strength. Which—he realized—Gabby had in spades. "Got too close to a bomb blast." At her gasp, he rushed on, "Only a concussion and some cracked ribs. I'll be back to active duty in a week."

"Oh, Clay." Her beautiful lips trembled as she put a hand gently on his rib cage. "And you still kicked in that window and fought so hard to…" Her eyes shone with tears.

Hope filled him. He pounced. "You *do* still have feelings for me."

She sucked in a breath, distanced herself by standing and going to look out the front window. "But you said my feelings weren't real. That I just had Savior Syndrome."

"And you said I didn't know myself as well as I thought. I think you were right."

Shrugging, she folded her arms across her chest and turned back to him. "Maybe it was Savior Syndrome. But, now *I* tried to help save *you*. So maybe we're even. Maybe we can be friends."

He gritted his teeth. "We're not just friends, and I can prove it." He got to his feet and took her into his arms, lowering his mouth to hers. He kissed her. Deep, ravenous kisses. "I don't deserve those feelings you have for me, but they're there." He put his lips on hers again. He wanted all of her. Her body. Her heart.

But she pulled away. "Why don't you deserve them?"

He stroked her long hair, trying to come up with a way out of this conversation. "I just never...did."

"Clay." That slightly scolding tone. "How can you believe that?"

He supposed if he wanted to have something more with her, something...real, then he'd have to *be* real.

Finally, he met Gabby's gaze. "One of my earliest memories is of my mom's boyfriend backhanding me across the face."

Gabby gasped. "Oh, Clay."

"After my mom married him, seemed like I got the belt, or the back of his hand every day. I ran away once. But I just got it worse when they found me and brought me home."

"I can't believe your mother let him do that."

He shook his head. "After I went to work at the quarry it mostly stopped. Guess he figured I was earning my keep then."

She rested her forehead on his shoulder, but he couldn't hold her right now. "My stepfather did me a favor."

"How can you say that?"

"Did you know the drop rate for BUD/S—that's SEAL training camp—is around 80 percent?"

Her eyes narrowed. "No."

"What they called Hell Week, I called a week. I'm a freakin' US Navy SEAL." He raised his brows. "But I haven't been home since I joined the Navy more than ten years ago."

"Clay." She caressed his cheek. "You may think your stepfather's treatment was the reason you made it through training, but that's not true. It's only because of you. You turned abuse into something good." She started pressing soft kisses along his jaw. Her arms had come around him, her fingers playing at the nape of his neck. Her gardenia scent surrounded him. Emotion welled up, feelings he hadn't let himself feel since he was a boy.

He pulled back, still holding her face between his palms. "I need you. I can't lose you. You see me, Gabby. I don't know how this whole love thing works. I don't know if I'll be any good at it. But when I woke up in that hospital in Kirkuk all I could think about was you in the hospital in Lucerne, and how you were there, holding my hand."

She blinked back tears.

"You think surviving the kidnapping made you brave, but it's the other way around. You survived the kidnapping *because* you're brave. You've never been afraid to go after what you really wanted. Even after you were threatened with death, you had the courage to not just go to that conference, but to laugh and twirl around a hotel room in pure joy.

"I want to be your kind of courageous, Gabby. And I want you to help me. You can have whatever parts of me that are worth anything. My heart, my soul…"

He dropped a brief kiss on her lips, took her hand from his neck and placed it on his chest. "Feel that heart pounding? It's never pounded like that for any other woman. Never constantly thought of a woman before either. No woman has ever risked her life for me. I love you, Gabby."

Her face crumpled as she smiled and cried at the same time. "And I love you, Clay Bellamy." She hugged him hard, and he welcomed the pressure on his ribs. Wanted to hold her forever.

She glanced up at him. "We can make this work, we'll do whatever it takes. I can look into banking jobs in Virginia Beach, if you…if you wanted—"

He grinned. "I want. But your career is important. We can do long-distance for a little while. I'll be relegated to desk duty in only a couple of years—"

"That reminds me. Did you know there's an organization for veterans called *Charlie Mike*?"

Clay frowned. "No."

"Veterans who still want to make a difference, go wherever there's a disaster or help is needed, they build homes, do amazing things."

Clay blinked. "Did I mention you're amazing?"

She gave a slow seductive smile. "Clay?"

Busy kissing her throat, he grunted, "Hmm?"

"Shall we…Charlie Mike?"

* * * * *

Look for other UNIFORMLY HOT! *romances from author Jillian Burns available from Harlequin Blaze at www.harlequin.com!*

COMING NEXT MONTH FROM

♦HARLEQUIN®
Blaze®

Available August 23, 2016

#907 HANDLE ME
Uniformly Hot!
by Kira Sinclair
Military K-9 handler Ty Colson has been lusting after his best friend's little sister for years. Now she's finally letting him into her bed, but will she ever let him into her heart?

#908 TEMPTED IN THE CITY
NYC Bachelors
by Jo Leigh
Tony Paladino is a licensed contractor who is Little Italy royalty. Catherine Fox hires Tony to renovate her downtown property. The attraction is fierce—and mutual. Too bad they're complete opposites!

#909 HOT SEDUCTION
Hotshot Heroes
by Lisa Childs
Serena Beaumont has always been the good girl, the one who wants a husband and kids. But when she rents a room to a notorious player, Hotshot firefighter Cody Mallehan, she's tempted to be very, *very* bad.

#910 NO LIMITS
Space Cowboys
by Katherine Garbera
Astronaut Jason "Ace" McCoy wasn't expecting to add *rancher* to his job title. Will a few sizzling weeks with his ranch co-owner, Molly Tanner, tempt him to give up the stars and stay in the saddle for good?

———————

HBCNM0816

REQUEST YOUR FREE BOOKS!
2 FREE NOVELS PLUS 2 FREE GIFTS!

HARLEQUIN®

Blaze

red-hot reads!

YES! Please send me 2 FREE Harlequin® Blaze® novels and my 2 FREE gifts (gifts are worth about $10). After receiving them, if I don't wish to receive any more books, I can return the shipping statement marked "cancel." If I don't cancel, I will receive 4 brand-new novels every month and be billed just $4.74 per book in the U.S. or $5.21 per book in Canada. That's a savings of at least 14% off the cover price. It's quite a bargain. Shipping and handling is just 50¢ per book in the U.S. and 75¢ per book in Canada.* I understand that accepting the 2 free books and gifts places me under no obligation to buy anything. I can always return a shipment and cancel at any time. Even if I never buy another book, the two free books and gifts are mine to keep forever.

150/350 HDN GH2D

Name	(PLEASE PRINT)	
Address		Apt. #
City	State/Prov.	Zip/Postal Code

Signature (if under 18, a parent or guardian must sign)

Mail to the **Reader Service:**
IN U.S.A.: P.O. Box 1867, Buffalo, NY 14240-1867
IN CANADA: P.O. Box 609, Fort Erie, Ontario L2A 5X3

Want to try two free books from another line?
Call 1-800-873-8635 or visit www.ReaderService.com.

* Terms and prices subject to change without notice. Prices do not include applicable taxes. Sales tax applicable in N.Y. Canadian residents will be charged applicable taxes. Offer not valid in Quebec. This offer is limited to one order per household. Not valid for current subscribers to Harlequin Blaze books. All orders subject to credit approval. Credit or debit balances in a customer's account(s) may be offset by any other outstanding balance owed by or to the customer. Please allow 4 to 6 weeks for delivery. Offer available while quantities last.

> **Your Privacy**—The Reader Service is committed to protecting your privacy. Our Privacy Policy is available online at www.ReaderService.com or upon request from the Reader Service.
>
> We make a portion of our mailing list available to reputable third parties that offer products we believe may interest you. If you prefer that we not exchange your name with third parties, or if you wish to clarify or modify your communication preferences, please visit us at www.ReaderService.com/consumerschoice or write to us at Reader Service Preference Service, P.O. Box 9062, Buffalo, NY 14240-9062. Include your complete name and address.

HBI5

SPECIAL EXCERPT FROM

HARLEQUIN Blaze

When military K-9 handler Ty Colson delivers retired war dog Kaia to her new owner, Van Cantrell's head wants nothing to do with the risk-hungry soldier determined to return to the front lines. But her body has other ideas...

Read on for a sneak preview of HANDLE ME, the first of Kira Sinclair's UNIFORMLY HOT! K-9 stories.

"I suggest you do exactly what I plan on doing and forget that night ever happened."

Van stared out at the neighborhood she called home. It was quiet. Nice. Full of professionals and families. She wanted to like it here, but honestly, it had never quite felt like home.

She felt him way before she heard him. All that pent-up tension and heat slipping over her skin like fingers, caressing her into a reaction she didn't want to feel.

Ty didn't actually touch her, though. He didn't have to.

"You keep telling yourself that, princess," he whispered, the soft puff of his breath tickling her ear. A shiver rolled down her spine. He was too close not to notice.

He chuckled.

Van ground her teeth together, though she wasn't sure if it was to bite back words or merely find another—safer—outlet for all that pent-up energy.

"I remember every moment of that night," he

murmured, his words low and dangerous to her equilibrium.

"Highly unlikely considering how drunk you were."

His fingertips found the curve of her neck and slowly, devastatingly trailed across her skin. Goose bumps erupted in the wake of his touch, a telltale sign she was powerless to hide.

"I stopped drinking the minute we hit that tree house. I was sober as a judge by the time things got…heated."

"Ha!"

"The way you looked, naked, flushed with desire and spread out on that blanket, is something I'll never forget. Not as long as I live." Ty swept her hair over one shoulder, exposing the curve of her neck. The warm summer breeze ghosted over her, replaced almost immediately by the blazing heat of his mouth.

She whimpered. The sound simply escaped, uncontrollable and way too revealing.

No. "I can't do this," she said, the words coming out a strangled mess. "You're the reason my brother is dead. He never should have been in Afghanistan. He followed *you* into that life. My body might think you're God's gift to continuing the species, but my brain doesn't give a shit."

Ty's gaze hardened, his eyes like ice. In that moment she could see the ruthless, fearless, dangerous soldier that he'd become. "Take Kaia inside and be sure to give her plenty of water." His voice was flat. "I'll be back tomorrow."

*Don't miss HANDLE ME by Kira Sinclair,
available in September 2016 wherever Harlequin®
Blaze® books and ebooks are sold.*

www.Harlequin.com

HBEXP0816

Reading Has Its Rewards

Earn **FREE BOOKS!**

Register at **Harlequin My Rewards** and submit your
Harlequin purchases from wherever you shop to earn
points for free books and other exclusive rewards.

Plus submit your purchases from now till May 30th
for a chance to win a $500 Visa Card*.

Visit **HarlequinMyRewards.com** today

Earn
FREE
REWARDS
Join
Today!
HarlequinMyRewards.com

MYRI6

Love the Harlequin book you just read?

Your opinion matters.

Review this book on your favorite book site, review site, blog or your own social media properties and share your opinion with other readers!